SHANE

DESTINY'S KEY

BY

W. SHANE WILSON

A FANTASY EPIC NOVEL

SHANE

SHANE

SPECIAL THANKS TO MY WIFE AND CHILDREN FOR THEIR FAITH IN ME AND THEIR LOVE OF MY TALES.

SHANE

SHANE

Distributed through LULU.com

First printing December 4, 2008
Book Printed in America (via digital printer)

ISBN: 978-0-578-00301-6

SHANE

SHANE

SHANE

SHANE

SHANE

I sit here in the sunshine of Lon's sky as my children run around me, reflecting on the events that have brought me to this place and time. Further, for the first time in nearly four years my heart and soul are at peace, however, the events leading up to this day are anything but peaceful, But let me start from the beginning so you too can reflect on the great journey that my life has take and how it affects you as well as myself.

One day four years ago I found myself hurtled mercilessly fifteen years in the future. Hard for you to believe how do you think it made me feel. Well I'll go back to where all the trouble began, it was July 1, 1995 and I was getting ready to go on vacation. My wife Anne and I were saying good-by to my son Justin and our newborn baby girl crystal. The trip was due to Anne's depression, she thought that having crystal made her get fat, and that she was going to stay that way. I decided to take her on a road trip to brighten her spirits. She agreed to go, so I made the necessary arrangements and off we went.

Our course took us from Vancouver Way. cross country state by state until we came by an outdoor rock concert in Colorado, so we decided to stop and listen. I parked the car near the wooded area so we could get out easy if we wanted to leave. Anne got out and stood by the car waiting for me to get my tired old butt out of the car. When I did get out of our new slick black Firebird, the music was bumping. Anne's toes were already tapping along to the band when I walked up to her. For the first time in months she was smiling, and I took that as a good omen. There were four bands scheduled to perform, two of which we really liked and two we had never heard of. Upon the departure of the

SHANE

second group we liked I found I had piss like a Russian
racehorse. A need no doubt you probably understand. Well this
is where my strange tale begins.

SHANE

SHANE

CHAPTER ONE: ENDINGS.

It was hot and dry so I told Anne to stand in the shade while I went into the nearby woods to urinate. I gave her a little kiss and said I'll be back in a minute. Green moss grew on the south sides of the trees where I entered the brush, which should of been the first clue but I missed it. I turned around periodically to see if the crowd could still see me from where I was standing. Farther and farther I walked from the concert area but, it always seemed that I was still in plain view of the crowd.

At this I decided I would walk straight into the woods for a little while then turn and looked, if I did not See anyone, I would urinate then walk back the way I came. So I that's exactly what I did. There was a big cedar tree just before me, no longer being able to hold back the overwhelming urge, I ran behind the tree and did my business. The trip back should of been a bloody snapola, yet it was not. Walking the same way back as I had come I realized, I was lost which was impossible, yet I was not on the same course as I had taken to get where I was now. I have a vivid sense of direction and have been a camper since I was a kid and in all that time I never got lost. I should make it back in only a minute or so, but I didn't.

Looking for any sign of tangible life I finally came to a small Town like place where I asked the first person I came to where I was and how to get back to where I came from. The man I asked

SHANE

was about six two and weighed near two hundred ten pounds. He was dressed strangely but it was getting late and Anne was probably worried sick about me.

I said pardon me sir, but I got lost in the woods and I need to get back to the field that the outdoor concert is being held in.

He said easy young fellow I can help you. At that point he took me to a hotel and said they will help you in there, have a nice day.

I also wished him well which I would later regret. I entered the hotel and the man behind the counter was also dressed very strangely but still I was determined to find my way home.

I went up too the counter and asked, can you tell me how to get back to the concert field?

He said yes. You just go out the back door of the hotel and follow the path around through the woods, here I'll show you son.

The man in the funny cloths led me to the back of the hotel where a door stood ajar waiting for me to burst through.

The man said I know your in a hurry but may I know your name before you go. Sean Savage , I replied.

He said goodbye and I reciprocated.

Once on the trail I found my way through the woods quite

SHANE

quickly, so quickly I was in the field in only a minute or less, which gave me the creeps because only moments ago I was in the deep woods and lost to boot. It was the place I had been only an hour before, yet there was not so much as a crumb on the ground to suggest that anyone had been there. Truly everyone including Anne was long gone.

   I spotted a pay phone near a drinking fountain on the far side of the parking lot so I ran over and slammed a quarter in the damn thing and it said please deposit fifty more cents, I remembered all my money was in the car. At this point I was madder than hell so I called my foster dad Jack.

Tye picked up the phone and said we don't want any, but I could hear Jack in the background say give me that phone.

  I said, jack thank God your home.

  He said who am I speaking Too.

  I said Sean.

  Jack paused only a brief moment then said if this is some kind-of
sick joke, I am not amused.

  Jack, I screamed cut the shit, I am not in the mood for any damn jokes.

He said Sean is that really you?

SHANE

Yes it's me, and I got separated from Anne, I replied.
Where are you at now Sean, Jack asked in haste?

Dossan Colorado, I told him.

Jack said, Stay put and I'll be there in about two hours.

OK, I said then we said bye and I waited.

Jack showed up in the time-frame he said he would and he
looked at me as looking at a dead person just reincarnated.

Then he blurted Sean my God it is really you?

Jack what's a matter with you I saw you only a couple of days
ago?

Jack has always been honest with me but I could feel that he
was stalling. He kept squirming all the way to the airport and
then on the plane too.

Did something happen to Anne that your trying to tell me, I
finally asked?

No, she's just fine. Sean you've been missing for fifteen years,
he said turning to me and nearly falling into tears at having to
bring the news.

O stop bull-shiting around and let's get home to our happy little

SHANE

families, I said trying to lift his spirits, but he looked very somber.

    We took an express flight to Portland, Oregon where I had just been a couple of days prior.

When I got off the plane, a man said your Sean Savage, hey I loved your book.

  What's he talking about Jack, I asked in confusion?

  We have a lot of things to discuss son, was his calm response.

  Jack did not utter a single word all the way to Ridgefield. Upon arrival I was greeted by tears from my whole foster family.

I began to yell at the top of my lungs will somebody please tell me what the hell is going on. Every time I see someone they act so strange it's beginning to give me the creeps so stop it and tell me what has happened.

  They all looked at me as if I had just sprouted a three iron from my head, and were trying not to stare at it.

  Sean you have been missing for fifteen years, Carol said in surprise at my confusion.

Don't you start that crap too, I barked at her. Carol please, you tell me why every person I meet is acting so weird.

She said follow me.

SHANE

We went into the house and she pulled out an album and showed me the newspaper articles on my mystery disappearance, they were dated fifteen years ago to the date I was sitting and reading them. I thought this is crazy I only got lost this morning, I must be in the Twilight Zone.

Tye said, its true look at Sean he hasn't age at all, I'm older than he is now.

As I looked around I saw that Tye was right, everyone had age but me. I went over and looked in the mirror to make sure I was OK. Youth still hung in my face like a banner of defiance. A moment passed and I was still immobile, then I wanted to know what had happened to my family.

Jack and Carol looked at each other for a time with a startled look on both of their faces.

I said where are my family, are they OK or what.

Jack said I think it would be wise to explain some things to you before you see your family again.

So tell me already the suspense is killing me, I said with absolutely no humor in my voice which is unusual for me because I'm such a joker.

Carol said I think you might want to sit for a minute while I tell you what's been happening these past fifteen years.

SHANE

When I was seated Jack began his delicate speech. Carol just sat down next to me and held my hand for moral support because she knew what was going to be said and she felt sorry for me.

Jack cleared his throat twice like a man about to testify against the mob.

He said I'll just give it to you straight, Anne has remarried and she is quite wealthy to boot.

I interjected by saying what about Justin and Crystal?

Justin was told you're dead and Crystal thinks that Chris is her father, Jack said as fast as the words would come out.

Why would she think my brother was her father, I demanded as if the answer wasn't already obvious?

Chris is Anne's husband Sean, Carol said!

I calmly said, Where do they live Jack.

You really don't want to go there do you, he asked trying to get me to hold off.

YES AND NOW! OK, I shouted.
I regained my wits and put my hand on Jacks shoulder, took one mammoth breath and let it out. Jack and Carol both took deep breaths now that the burden of truth was lifted from their

SHANE

shoulders and the ball was in my court. I was visibly miffed so
They held the tongues until something needed to be said to break
the silence.

I'll take you over there but first I have something for you, Jack
said turning me toward the door.

We went outside and Jack walked up to a tarped car and pulled
the tarp off of the car. It was my old 77, Firebird.

I stood there smiling, because this was the first good thing that
had happened to me lately.

Frankly, It might have just made the difference between a blind
rage and simple fury, none-the-less I was happy for this brief
wonder.

Anne said I could have it, but I never let anyone drive because it
broke my heart to think of you as gone, Jack told me.

Thanks for keeping good care of my ride, do you have the keys
to this baby Dad, I asked?

Yes, I got the keys right here, he said.

Good then we'll take my car to visit, I blurted with a twisted grin
that made him nervous!

Jack gave me directions to Anne's humble little home, which
was a far cry from being humble. I got out went up to the door

SHANE

and knocked. A moment later the door opened and a well built young man stood before me smiling.

He said yes can I help you?

 I just stood there not knowing what to say, this was my son and boy had he grown.

Then all of a sudden the young man asked haven't we met before? The boy spotted Jack behind me.
He said grandpa what are you doing here?

Jack did not reply, he only pointed at me. So the boy faced me again because I was staring at him.

So this is how you turn out, I said.

 The young man began to get nervous, and said what do you want here?

I replied, I want back what is mine.

 Yes, what's that, he asked me?

Everything your uncle Chris stole from me, I grunted in anger.

Justin came closer and looked me hard in the face then said I know you don't I?

O'yes Justin you know me, I told him.

SHANE

A light seemed to come on in Justin's eyes all of a sudden. My mom has pictures of you in her bedroom on the dresser in the corner. HEY, wait a damn minute those pictures are of my dad. Justin stood looking at an imaginary portrait for it seemed like an eon.

Suddenly he said, you're my father aren't you.

I said yes I am.

Just at that moment Crystal said who are you talking to Justin?

Come and see, Justin said to his little sister.

She approached the door slowly and looked around. There was no revelation from her such as Justin had made probably because she was to young to have remembered me.

She said hi I'm Crystal, who are you?

Before I was able to answer the question Justin broke in by saying he's our father.

Crystal said very funny, mom and dad are in their bedroom.

I said is that so and push past Crystal, she grabbed my arm and pulled saying you can't come into someone's house without being invited.

SHANE

I pushed her off of my arm and began into the house, she went to cartwheel kick me in the back but I turned and swept her feet out from under her.

Justin grabbed Crystal's arm and said stay the hell out of his way for a little while because he really is your father. Crystal just looked totally confused at her brother as if he just lost mind.

Jack came in and said that Justin was telling the truth and it was best to stay away from the firing line.

I walked up to a door where I could hear the sounds of lovemaking, and I kicked that door off of it stinking hinges. Chris started to get up but I kicked him in the face so hard he flipped upside down, and Anne was reaching for the gun I gave her years ago.

So this is how you two repay me huh. At that moment they looked at me and both just froze not knowing if I was real or a ghost or what.

Get your asses out of bed I want to talk to both of you, I growled.

They watched as I turned and left the room. Jack and my kids were down stairs when I got there waiting to find out what happened. There was no surprise when I told them to get comfortable because it was going to be a bumpy ride, so we went into the living and sat waiting for Chris and Anne to arrive. After a very brief period of time they walked into the room.
Crystal jumped up and ran to Anne and said this horrible man

SHANE

said he is my real father.

Anne said that's because, and she pause looked at me very carefully then said he is.

Crystal looked to Chris for some moral support, but found none.

Chris said is it really you Sean?

I didn't answer that question because the answer was in plain view and Crystal was staring at me for the first time as if asking herself is this man part of me, do I have something of him in me. I returned my attention back to Chris.

How long have you been married, I asked?

Fourteen and a half years, Chris replied.

You bitch, you married my own brother after only six months of my disappearance, And you, sorry bastard dare to lay your filthy hands on my wife when I'm barely gone, how come my daughter doesn't know anything about me, and why did you tell Justin I was dead when I am not, I yelled in a near rampage?

Chris said is it you Sean or am I having a dream?

If you think this is a dream then look in the mirror at the bruise I gave you.

Justin asked, where you been dad, I mean sense you haven't

SHANE

been around for a long time you know?

 Well Justin I was just where your mom left me, at the concert in Colorado. I explained what had happened and that's when they noticed for the first time I had not aged at all.

 So what now dad, asked my son?

 Hell I don't know, say how did you afford this house, it's a mansion for Pete sake, I asked in a calmer tone.

 Chris spoke this time, it came from the book you finished before you went on that trip fifteen years ago, he said hanging his head.

 What do you mean, I asked?

 Your book sold five million copies, so we were rich, and that's how we got the house, he explained.

 So you robbed me too. I gotta go but I'll come back later and finish with you, I told them.

 I called and the publisher of my book from Jack's home, he said he was going to get on a plane and fly as fast as he to see me.

I made a quick visit to the bank where I was cheered for my book. The bank president said all the money was still in my name, so I put all of it in a new private account to protect my interests.

SHANE

Jack said, hey Sean I'm starving let's get some food.

OK, I buy after all I'm a millionaire you know, I laughed out loud.

We stopped at a restaurant that looked good in Hazel Dell. While we ate someone recognized me and called the news and suddenly we were surrounded by reporters. Are you Sean Savage the writer of Skyfire the best selling book in the last ten years.

Fifteen, I said.

What did you say, the woman asked me?

I said fifteen years ago I wrote that book.

Sorry Mr. Savage, I was wrong, she said.

No problem miss, I am not perfect either so we'll go easy on each other, I told her with a smile.

Where have you been for so long, and why is this the first time we have ever seen you in person, she asked.

I don't think I could explain even if I wanted to, but I will say this I am going to write another book soon, look for it, I said.

Are you still married to Anne, she asked?

No comment, I told her with a frown at the thought.

26

SHANE

After a time we finish eating and answering questions so we took off.

   On the way home Jack said, what are you going to do? I know you, and for you this is only a couple of days and to everyone else it has been years. I know your being calm, but what are you going to do? If I came home and Carol had a new husband and my kids were as big as me, I think I would go crazy.

   Daddio cool your jets, before you over heat your motor, I'm going to be fine but I am going to have to do something that's for damn sure. What I haven't the foggiest notion, but something that's for sure, I said.

   Mayse the youngest son who is now to look at older than I am, was standing in the driveway waiting for us. Phone Sean.

   Thanks bud, I said running for the phone, it was Brian Fuser my publisher asking if he could drop in right away too discuss some important business.

I said yes of course, then asked Carol if she minded.

   Brian showed up at seven and began almost immediately to get to the topics he thought needed covering. He started with book royalties, then asked for the other book he was promised. I asked him who promised him the second book, and he said Anne who else.

SHANE

Who else I said, as I looked at Jack. Brye I have been missing for fifteen years, there is no other book!

WHAT, I have been waiting for five years for the hell of it, Brian said?

Yes, I told him, but I am going to write another book so it'll be okay..

One month later I had already bought the biggest house in the county, which happen to be in Ridgefield. The car and boat I purchased for the hell of it. Loud knocking erupted from my front door so I ventured forth to find whom was pulverizing my front door. I opened the door and there was Justin.

Hey dad, what's up, Justin said?

Hey yourself stranger, come in, I said with a big smile.

He came in and sat down in my coliseum sized front room.

Dad, mom is worried that your going to sue her and she'll loose her house and all the money she's enjoyed.

Well what do you think I should do son, I asked him in earnest?

Don't take everything away just to hurt mom, that's what I think, Justin said.

I am going to take the money away, but the house is hers so she

28

SHANE

can keep it, I told my son.

   Justin said I knew you were a good guy and wouldn't leave mom
flat. Dad can I move in with you, I mean I barely know you and I
don't want that to continue any longer.

   First, you need to get your mothers approval and while you are
gathering that, take her a message for me. The message said
she and Curt were to meet me in A. Shilo Attorney at law on the
second day of the week. Justin displaced for home.

   I began to reflect on just how lonely I was and found that the
prospect of my son living with me was very a shining one. Upon
the second day of the month, I was joined by my brother and my
wife in the office of my attorney A. Shilo.

   You were asked to come here upon the request of my client
Sean Savage. First of all we will address the matter of Mrs.
Savage's bigamy. Since you married the brother of your first
husband who you are still legally married, you are in violation of
the law and can be put in prison if my client wishes. However he
does not wish it so, we will address item two which my client has
not over looked. The book he wrote and you got rich off! You
have bought new cars, a big house and a great boat, well against
my advice you may keep all of your shit, Although the money has
already been taken back into the custody of the rightful owner.
Item three, you are to be given three and a half million dollars to
maintain the life style that the children were brought up in. Item
four, each of the children are to be given ten million dollars each
as of the seventh day of this month, the person who will govern

SHANE

the accounts will be Sean himself until the kids turn twenty one or graduate from college. Last order of business is for Anne to sign the divorce papers, said Shilo in one great breath.

Anne stood up and said I think I should get a little more money than that, don't you think?

Shilo broke in suddenly by reminding her she was a felon and could legally receive nothing but jail time. Anne signed the settlement papers and was about to leave.

I said oh by the way Justin is going to live with me. She gave me a glance but said nothing.

Justin moved in the next Friday. Once I realized that my boy didn't have a car I asked why. He said it was because his mom didn't want him gone all the time.

That's bullshit what kind of a car do you want, I asked?

I would really like a BANSHEE, but mom said I would only wreck it then she would by out a hundred grand.

Justin do I have to remind you that you're a millionaire now and you can buy any damn thing you want, I added! And What is a Banshee, I thought it was an ATV?

So I can have a BANSHEE, Justin said with excitement? Well, it is a hand made 600 horsepower roadster, made by a Germany engineer living in Seattle.

SHANE

I said, Yes, why not?

Justin said, cool and hugged me so hard I thought my ribs would crack.

I said when would you like to go get your new car?

He said right now!

That afternoon when we got back a beautiful young girl was in the driveway. The girl walked right up to the car, Justin rolled down the window and she canted through the window and she kissed all over my son's visage. The stunning young woman was so engulfed that she did not realize I was even there.

Justin said let me park and then I'll introduce you to my father. Justin parked the car got out just in time to be grappled by the lovely girl.

Jeanie give me a second, I missed you to but, Justin said, before he could utter a single word more she was on him again, this time he didn't fight it. I managed to guide the love starved youths into my house somehow. I left them alone, it seemed to be the right idea. Hours later Justin sprang forth in the happiest mood I have ever seen, obviously he just got laid, but I asked anyway.

Did you want to tell me anything like if you move in you'll be sleeping with your pretty girlfriend, I poked at him?

SHANE

A voice from behind me said it isn't nice for a friend to ask about someone else's sex life.

I said, you are right but, I own this house and I'm Justin's father.

For a moment she said nothing then she exclaimed I should have known who you were because Justin has never let anyone ask him questions like that before.

Well Justin what is this little ball of fire's name, I asked?

Jeanie, he said with a great deal of pride.

Kids I thought to myself, how different they are now. I did not see my son or his lover the rest of the day. Six o'clock rolled around and I was sitting in my study reading because I love to read when Jeanie came into my study.

She said may I speak with you?

Of course honey, come in and sit and talk with me.
She was wearing only a blue tee-shirt and nothing more. It fit the contours of her perfect body, being tightest over her firm medium size breasts. When she sat down she pulled the shirt up so not to sit on it, but as she did so she exposed all of her body below her belly button.

I said I can see why my son is in love with you. You have a great body and a beautiful face. So what do you want to talk about? I

32

SHANE

had a hard time listening while my eyes surveyed her property
and boy was her property worth allot!

   Jeanie said Justin and I started making love in seventh grade
and have had a healthy, yet secret sex life. We are both nearly
eighteen and I want to know if you
mind our sex life in your house?

   If you want the truth sweetheart if Justin wasn't sleeping with
you as sexy as you are I would.

   She smiled and said I think you're cute also, but I love Justin
and I want to marry him.

WHEN?

   She said what do you mean when?

   I said just that when do you want to get hitched?

   We really haven't thought much about it, we thought we would
probably get married when could afford it.

   Laughing almost out of control I said didn't Justin tell you?

   She said tell me what?

   That he's a millionaire now of course, I said. She jumped
up and started running for the stairs so I followed her. Jeanie
went straight for Justin's room, opened the door.

33

SHANE

Jeanie asked Justin who was still half asleep, are you a millionaire now?

   Justin said, o'yeah that, I must of forgot to mention it or something.

     Morning came to the sounds of my son and my soon to be Daughter-in-law jumping on the bed or play some kind of game. I regressed to the kitchen like Neanderthal man in search of prey to appease my voracious appetite. Reality slapped me in the froth and yelled, you cretin if you don't shop you don't feast!

Justin get your pants on and come down here, I hollered!

   OK, I'll be down in a sec dad. Jeanie showed up before Justin in a towel.

   We got to stop meeting like this it's hard on my heart, I said.

   She giggled then said I think I know how to help you.

   I asked, What do you mean by that?

   You'll see she said. Justin then arrived with a happy dumb look on his face.

   Hey dad, what's up, he yawned?

   We do not have chow in the house to eat and we need to seize

SHANE

some or starve. I want you and Jeanie to cloth your bodies and fetch
the groceries for our humble home.

 Humble home,(pause) Justin said OK we'll go presently, as soon as Jeanie gets dressed. Yes, about that does she always walk around nearly naked, I asked?

 Yes, she's proud of her body, Justin said with a dumb grin.

 Well it is making my hormones dance everything I see her half dressed, I told him.

 Jeanie told me she talked with you in your study when I was asleep wearing only a small tee-shirt and you were honest about what you thought about her body and her in general, he explained.

You were not upset by what I said?

 No dad, I know that you would never jeopardize my happiness.

 Well I thought about it though Justin and I got to tell you hold on to that girl, she all full of piss-n-vinegar, I said with a wink. Justin just laughed.

 After breakfast was wiped out, we realized we had no plains for the day. Many ideas flew between Justin and I, but Jeanie just sat and smiled.

SHANE

Justin said where do you think we should go baby?

Jeanie said we're going to the sea for a couple of days to take in the sights, then she nudged Justin as if he knew what was going on.

The ocean was not a good prospect to me but since the trip was for all of us I went along for the ride. We packed our stuff for half the day, finally we were ready to go. I brought around my custom built Ford Truck. All the luggage was loaded and the security alarm was set, so off we went. The stereo was bumping going down the highway, it seemed that our taste in music was about the same.

Sol was beating on the earth in full glory. Green trees or shrubs were everywhere, it was going to be a good day after all. Sounds of the ocean rang in the air about us. I stopped the Ford to watch a school of killer whales go by. Justin and Jeanie seemed to also share my basic taste in most things, such as music, food, clothes, movies, people. Once we remounted the truck we pressed ever forth to our destination, the ocean by some lighthouse she kept mentioning. That should have been a clue but I played dumb just to be safe. It was nearly dark when we finally made contact with the place Jeanie want to arrive at. IT was a beautiful old lighthouse. I drove in by the other standing buildings were it seemed that suitable parking was meant to be.

Jeanie said, pointing to a red door-ed building, is where we will stay. The other one is the galley.

SHANE

Who runs this place, I asked, don't you think we should find them and let'm know we're here, I asked her?

Jeanie pointed to the lighthouse and said Nick already knows we're here Sean.

Jeanie went into the lighthouse after giving Justin and I careful instructions.

Hey Justin, you ever been here before something gives me the feeling Norman Bates is going to jump out of a shadow yelling mother, ill get these foolish lodgers, I said making funny faces and stabbing gestures. Justin was just wailing at this point.

Stop it I can't breath, You're so funny, he choked out.

Yes well if you wake up with a psycho in your face yell to me so I can make a run for it, and don't stand in front of the truck because I'll run you down on my way out, I told him.
At that we both had a good laugh.

Dad, you know I think I'm going to have a great life with you, because you're so off the wall, he said.

Justin remember I was lost in time for fifteen years, so physically I am only seven years older than you, so we should have a lot in common. We unloaded the Ford into the rooms they we were told then walked down by the ocean. To our surprise there was a beach.

SHANE

It was man made but no less a really great beach. I said
Justin let's go skinny dipping.

He said major idea bud!

Water rolled over us as we body surfed naked in the unusually
warm ocean that seem to have no rock around, yet it had bitchin
waves crashing in on the beach. Our fun was suddenly
interrupted by a voice we didn't recognize.

It said this is not a nude beach.

I said there isn't anybody else around so we think anyone
would mind, our mistake. We got out of the water and got
dressed
but still did not see the person the voice came from.

Justin said I wonder what happened to Jeanie? I don't know,
but that Bates motel thing is starting back up.

Tell me about it said Justin.

We walked up the bank and around to where the buildings were.
We were passing the galley and noticed the smell of good food
was coming from within.

Justin stepped forward and I said remember uncle norm and
made a stabbing motion. He nodded then both of us went into
the galley. Hot steaming dishes of yummy

SHANE

looking foods. Looking carefully around we did not take any just in case it was bad manners. Justin pointed off to our left, I saw a door and we both heard noise so we went to investigate. A moment before Justin and myself could enter Jeanie came forth and suggested we eat, because she was I'm starved.

Jeanie showed Justin and I where to wash up for dinner. Feasting was now cardinal on our minds.

Sean sit here, said Jeanie. Justin you sit here by me so I can fondle you, said Jeanie. There were four chairs at the table which we sat at. Jeanie said that she looked for us but guessed we had gone for a walk and started the meal.

Then who yelled at us down by the beach, I made the Norman bates stabbing gesture and Justin
shivered.

Where is this Nick, are we going to wait for him to come and eat, I asked. Jeanie shook her head no and we ate.

I ate enough to choke a pig I said.

So did I dad, said Justin.

You'll work it off tonight baby, said Jeanie.

OOH, we both said and all three of us started laughing. The table and dishes were cleaned and put away.

SHANE

At that point Jeanie said to Justin it's time to work mister, so let's go.

I said goodnight and we parted.

My room was a bit cool so I started a fire in the fireplace. The fire was blazing along when saw something or someone go by my window, I could hear Justin and Jeanie making love next door so I knew it wasn't them. I got up and dressed quickly and went out to investigate. The figure was going down toward the ocean, so I followed it. The path wound around from the left and then right the rest of the way to the beach. The figure was just in sight, when it reached the beach I hid behind a big rock. The figure walked into the sand stopped and disrobed. The figure was now a very beautiful naked young woman, who rubbed her naked body all over with her hands as if trying to work out the stiffness. She stood in that spot for a moment letting the wind blow in her face and over her body. She moved to the water, put one foot in the ocean and seemed satisfied. The ocean swallowed her up as she dove into it. I watched her for a very long time just swimming around. Suddenly, I got an idea. I crept down on the beach and took the girls clothes. Being as quiet as I could I crept back into the veil of darkness.

SHANE

SHANE

CHAPTER TWO: BEGINNINGS

The night was warm so I didn't feel the least bite bad about taking the girls clothes, after all it was warm out here by the ocean tonight. I was once again behind the giant boulder in who's shadow I had hid in early on in this night. The girl ventured forth from the water to find no apparel on the beach were she left it. She looked around to see if the wind had blown them down the shore or something. Of course she nothing, because her clothes were folded neatly under my arm waiting for her to come looking for them. At first she appeared to be angry at the loss of her clothes, but then the angry assured look on her face faded away and she seemed genuinely afraid. I almost said don't worry your in no danger, but she was running right for my spot. The girl sprinted past me so fast she did not even see me standing there. I followed her to the lighthouse itself, which she ran into and closed the door. Curious, I thought. Jeanie never said that Nick had a beautiful girl here with him.

I approached the door and knocked. The girl answered the door in only a hand towel, which showed most of her lovely form.

Who the hell are you, she said?

I am the guy who found your clothes, I said and at that moment I held out the clothing to her. She could not take them without disgarding the towel she was trying to cover her body with. I stepped forward and she jumped back.

Relax, honey I'm only going to rap your shirt around you, I said!

42

SHANE

Ok, but you watch your step pal, she said as menacing as she could!

I put the girls shirt around her and buttoned it up, then reached under her shirt and pulled the towel out, she just looked mad for a moment then smiled.

Thank you, she said.

No biggy, I told her. She then invited me in for a cup of Jo. She disappeared into another room and a short time later she returned with two cups of coffee. She was still in only the shirt I had put on her naked torso. The pert little grin on her face was welcome in my eyes because she was so beautiful. I smiled back, like a hungry wolf.

DO you always still a girls clothes just so you can meet her, she asked with a little smile?

That obvious huh, I said sheepishly?

I saw you on the beach watching me and then you swiped my clothes, she told me.

Sorry, didn't intend to be so clumsy in my attempt to meet you, I said.

Her smile grew again and she said, Well, now that you have seen me up close what do you think?

SHANE

You are Ravishing, I slobbered out!

The girls face turned a bit red then she smiled and said your very hansom you know.

Your only saying that in defense, I quickly added.

Actually, I thought you were cute when I open the door, but I was not sure if I could trust you to be a gentlemen in-lieu of my delicate situation.

I laughed out loud and said I'm no gentleman sweetheart I just wanted to see you up close naked if you want the truth.

You are very honest, Say who are you, she asked?

Don't you know, I inquired?

If I knew who you were I think I wouldn't have asked, don't you think, she said?

Why should I tell you who I am when I don't know who you are, and where is this Nick who is suppose to be running this place, I said?

She gave me a strange look, but said nothing.

Well we seem to like each other that is obvious she said.

44

SHANE

Yes ,so what now I said?

I could asked you to spend the night, if you'll behave your self, she said.

I ask her if she would like to explain what she meant by behave myself?

She said that she would like me to stay but did not want to be mauled.

Well, what do you want me to do this evening darling, I asked?

Smiling, she said I want to be held and caressed until I fall to sleep.

I would be very happy to be your teddy bear tonight. At that I walked over and lifted her and asked where is your bedroom honey?

She pointed to a room on the far right of the first floor then place her tiny face in the crick of my neck. I made a beeline for her room, kicked the door open and came to the side of her bed, stopped and put her on her feet. She looked at me with a little surprise. I smiled and then began unbuttoning her shirt which was her only article of clothing. She looked a little scared but she smiled and undressed me. To her great surprise, I only laid her gently back onto the bed. She had the most incredible body I had ever seen and it was mine for the taking. I opted to gently massage her body until she relaxed. I began kissing her body at

45

SHANE

her toes, making my way up her body just as slow as I could to
prolong the stimulation. She moaned and giggled as I ran my
tongue and lips over her tender areas. When I finally reached her
mouth she had already experienced complete relaxation and we
had not had intercourse. She laid me down and began to
massage my back and they rest of me until I grabbed her into my
arms and held her firmly in my grasp. She relaxed in my arms
like a person who feels safe and loved...

 We crept into her soft warm bed and fell into each others
waiting arms without a single word. We fell asleep on
and off over the length of the night. I chose to only gently
kiss the night away for the beautiful naked girl in my arms
instead of giving her a night of incredible sex and passion
to remember in the morning.

 When the morning finally arrived, she was already awake and
she was staring at me as I slept.

 Good morning lover she said.

 I'm hardly your lover since I didn't ravage you daring.

Well you know what I mean. I am dying to know who you are,
your the guy I have been waiting for.

I offered all of myself to you
on a silver platter and you didn't take it all at once, you are
savoring me, as if I'm to precious to waste or rush. I could fall
for someone as beautiful as you in second, but I would like to

SHANE

have more than a nights worth of passion to remember you by,
that's why I did not have full blown sex with you last night.

There is another reason, but it's personal and if you stay in my
life long enough, you'll have it all. I want to be your lover but not
just today but forever, because I have loved and lost before.

  She said then let us plan on forever.

  Are you sure you can tell that I'm the right man for you.

  YES, O YES, there is no doubt in my heart or mind that your
prince charming from another time and place.

  You don't know just how right you are, I said.

  We got out of bed as slow as honey drops and showered
together most of the morning.

  Jeanie came into the lighthouse and said say Nick have you
seen Justin's dad?

  The girl in my arms yelled, he's not in here.

Nick, I quizzed? The girl said yes. Your Nick?

  Yes, why are you looking at me like that for, she said.

  I thought Jeanie said Nick was a man. How do you know
Jeanie?

SHANE

She is my son's live in lover, who he plans to marry.

Your son, she asked?

Yes, I answered.

Wait, who the hell are you, she asked while chewing on my ear?

I am Sean SAVAGE, millionaire, I own a mansion and a yacht, I answered through clinched teeth.

That is not possible your way to young to be Justin's dad.

Get dressed Nicky my love and we will explain everything over breakfast, I told her.

WE, what do you mean we, Nick asked.

You will understand later what I meant by we, I said.

Justin was already eating his breakfast when we reached the galley.

Hey dad, where you been, I was a little worried when you weren't in your cabin.

Nicky just stood there with a dumbfounded look on her face. I motioned to sit and grab a bite. Over the course of the morning meal I with the help of Justin and Jeanie, explained the way I

48

SHANE

had been cheated out of fifteen years of my life, but by the same token I am still a young man. In the beginning Nicky kept looking at Jeanie to see if this were some kind of sick joke, but Jeanie only indicated that it was all true. Nicky was in total disbelief most of the story, yet the weight of the story alone kept her from stopping the tale going on. I let Justin fill in the details that I didn't know which helped Nicky to believe the terrific fairytale we unfolded carefully to make Nicky understand how I came to be so young, in spite of my chronological age. Nicky sat holding my hand not knowing if it was a joke or a simple twist of fate.

   When I finally finished the story Nicky took my hand and said that Jeanie was trying to fix me up with her.

 Jeanie said that you were Justin's dad, so I guessed that you were an old guy so I stayed out of sight so didn't have to meet you.

 Well now you have met me what do you think of me sugar, I asked?

 I like you too much for words to describe and I glad you came here I've been so lonely after. . . .

After what Nicky, I wanted to know?

 I don't think I am ready to talk about it Sean, she said.

    The day was warm and beautiful and Justin talked the rest of us into going jet skiing on the ocean. I went to my room

SHANE

and grabbed my gear, put on some outrageous trunks for swimming that Jeanie talk me into buying on the way up. Then I walked up to the lighthouse to see what Nicky was going to wear and I went in and she was just pulling up the smallest one piece bathing suit I have ever seen on a woman.

 Nicky turned, looked at me and smiled and said I haven't worn this hot little number in awhile. I stared, and although it covered all of her goodies, the better part of most of her breasts were bare except for her nipples, and the back was a thong. There are only a few girls with a body good enough to wear this suit, and Nicky and Jeanie were both built more than good enough to pull this slinky little suit onto their torsos.

 Your so beautiful Nicky, I don't know when I have ever seen a more complete woman in my life, your pretty, smart and have a body that men would kill for, I told her. And a gentleness that she could not hide. I don't know why we became so close so fast, but we were drawn together like twin stars, I did not want to love her, my heart was sore and miserable still from all of the recent weirdness.

 She said o your just saying that because you want to make love to me.

 I said, I would be a fool if I did not.

 Nicky put a long shirt over herself and said lets go.

 The four of us reached the place that Justin had in mind for the

50

SHANE

jet skiing and he and I began unloading the truck. Jeanie pulled
off her shirt and she was wearing the same bathing suit type but
a different color. Nicky also shucked her shirt, and the two
of them went down on the beach and laid on their shirts. There
were other people on the beach but Justin and I weren't paying
attention. A couple of guys noticed how sexy Nicky and Jeanie
were dressed and came over and started talking to them.

One of them said hey you ladies looking for some action or
maybe a gangbang babe.

Jeanie said take a walk jerk.

   The guy said look whore your going to go with us whether you
like it or not and if your good I might even make you come bitch,
what is it going to be? Then he reached down and grabbed
Jeanie the other two grabbed Nicky and started walking away. I
saw what was happening and elbowed Justin it. We both ran
down the beach to where they were.

 I snuck up, behind them and I hit the guy holding Nicky's right
arm in the throat so hard I cracked his neck, the other guy threw
a roundhouse punch and I caught his arm and broke it the way I
was taught in my gung fu gwoon. Justin was right in front of the
guy who was trying to kidnap his girlfriend.

  The guy pushed her away and then hit her saying I didn't want
that whore anyway. Justin jumped forward grabbed the guy by
the throat with one hand and picked him up. Justin who is
incredibly cock strong began to clamp down on his neck, which

51

SHANE

was turning the guy's head dark purple. The guy's feet were
dangling four inches off the ground and at first they were kicking
violently, but now they were limp. Justin was gritting his teeth
so hard blood was trickling out of his mouth and down his cheek.

I said, Hey don't kill him son, just mess him up some.

   OK, Justin growled.

   Justin turned him around, so his back was forward, then he
lifted the guy up until he looked like he was laying on a bed. With
one powerful thrust of his knee fractured the back of his enemy
with a crunching sound like walking on potato chips. The damage
was not the permanent kind, but it was really painful anyway.
Justin was in a wild rage. I have seen it in myself and was afraid
for him, you can get lost if you don't try to retain your humanity.

   The three guys who wanted to sample the pleasures of our
woman were almost dead from the thrashing we had
administered happily. One laid on his back trying to get air
through his crushed windpipe, the second had both of his legs
broken and the bones were stinking out of his skin. Jerk number
three I savored more than the first two, because he was the one
who grabbed Nicky first, so I broke his buddies up before him to
put the fear of God in him. He soiled himself before I started on
him, breaking each and ever one of his ribs one at a time until he
coughed up blood, and began to choke out pleads of mercy.

Jeanie said it's obvious where you get your combat skills from to
Justin.

SHANE

Nicky was shaking so hard in my arms that I said calm down baby nobody will ever harm you as long as I live. She looked up into my eyes and said I have never been so afraid that you wouldn't be there to save me from those trash. I don't know if I want to ever make you angry after the way you destroyed those guys here on the beach.

I am a 4th degree black belt in **KAJUKENBO GUNG FU** and Justin is a first degree in the same art. I will teach if you want to learn.

Your so amazing Sean I love you, Nicky said then she kissed me.

Thank you miss, we train for just such an emergency as that. But, truth be told anger fuel those boys demise, I said.

The ocean was calm, the wind was blowing gently and the sun was just hot enough to deep tan the hot girl I was falling in love with. Justin and Jeanie were splashing each other as they sped around the bay.

The sun crawled over the horizon into the night and Justin and I loaded up the jet skis while the girls walked down the beach hand and hand talking about something, however Jeanie had her 25calibur Beretta pistol in her other hand.

Justin suddenly said, those are hands down the sexiest women on earth.

I agree they are the best there is, good bodies and better hearts

SHANE

yes we are a couple of lucky bastards for sure.

 On a rock down the beach the girls sat down and held each other close and they started hugging, but they were to far for Justin or me to see them undress out of their outerwear and went for a swim.

    Justin stayed in the truck to warm it up and I walked down the beach in search of our ladies. I walked into a large group of rocks, behind one I saw Nicky and Jeanie laying in the sand. Jeanie was hugging Nicky. I hid behind a rock and watched. Nicky pushed Jeanie upright and changed position. After a short time they disengaged from one another. They must have resolved whatever they were talking about.

 Jeanie and Nicky walked up to the truck hand in hand saying that they hoped we were ready to go because they were hungry as bulls. I just smiled stupidly at them. Nicky looked a little nervous when she noticed the look on my face. The ride home was a quiet one that's only sounds were the radio and kissing.

 Night fell hard upon us as we arrived back at the lighthouse. Nicky and Justin started unloading the truck, while I went down to walk on the beach. I roamed down the beach for probably about a mile, then I simply stopped and sat on a small rock facing the ocean. Elsewhere in the galley, Justin was cooking up some food with the help of a very quiet Nicky.

 Why so quiet sugar, still thinking about those trash on the beach?

SHANE

Nicky said no, I mean I was not really thinking about that. Justin is it wrong to love two people, I mean I don't love them both at the same time.

I loved one in the past and I think I love one now.

Nicky started crying all of a sudden and was talking nonsense that Justin could not understand. Justin walked over and put a arm around her.

Stop crying Nicky and tell old Justin your troubles child.

Down on the beach the waves crashed gently, the wind blow about 15 mph, the moon in the heavens was a blue man with whom I would reflect upon my life with. Yet he had no comfort to offer me this night or any other, but I find that just being there with him would make my heart lighter somehow. I fell into tears as I had many times, though I knew I would not be able to endear if I did not do so.

Jeanie walked down the beach in search of me. I was so caught up in my own thoughts that I did not see Jeanie walk by.

Justin had Nicky drinking some rum to help her relax.

She drank it down and held out her glass to be filled again. Justin filled the glass with the rum I brought with me encase I could not find any up where we were going.

Nicky said Justin what happened when your dad showed up, I

SHANE

mean how did everybody react to him being back after being lost for fifteen years?

Justin said, don't you mean how did my mother react?

Yes, that is what I wanted to know.

Well! She was scared to death he would kill her because she married my uncle Chris six months after my father disappeared. My dad is a 4th degree black belt in **KAJUKENBO GUNG FU** after all and he was U.S. full contact light weight champion. I have been trying to capture his title myself for about two years, Justin explained.

Is it a hard thing to do, win this championship, Nicky asked?

Yes, very hard and my dad won it at the rank of only student black belt. He held it until he came up missing, Justin told her.

Then is he still the champ since he has not lost his title to anyone, said Nicky?

No, they had a tournament to decide the person who would be his successor, Justin grunted in disgust at the words.

Well where are you in line for the title, Asked Nicky as the tears stopped?

Justin said, I am ranked number six in line for a shot for the belt.

SHANE

Nicky asked, Why doesn't Sean go get his title back?

Nicky, I don't think he has thought about it since he showed up, was Justin's answer.

I sitting in the shadow of a large rock when I saw Jeanie Walking down the beach.

I said, Hey, where are you off to?

Jeanie turn with a start, who said that?

I did, over here in the shadow of this big rock, I said.

Sean is that you, Jean asked?

Yes it is and why are you down here instead of with that handsome son of mine darling, I inquired?

She said, I have noticed that you seem to be very lonely and that it must be hard to loose your life and wife, kids all at once. So, I brought you here to meet Nicky who also lost all of her family at once. The difference is you got some of them back, she can't hers are dead.

Jeanie that still doesn't answer why you are here on the beach now, I said while looking at the ocean rolling in.

Jeanie said, I saw you today on the beach watching Nicky and I holding each other.

57

SHANE

Why didn't you stop when you saw me, I asked?

Because if you didn't know that I saw you, then we could finish our talk and Nicky would feel better.

Is that the first time you have done that Jeanie, I asked with a grin?

No, I use to live next door to Nicky when we were kids, she moved a year ago, and until then we were lovers, she said.

Did Justin know about this, I had to know?

Jean said, All Justin knows is that he was my first man.

Then tell me if you have been lovers with Justin since seventh grade, which is way to damn young, how long have you and Nicky been lovers, I said?

Jean smiled and said, Since ninth grade.

Why would you do that if you had Justin, I asked?

Nicky is the most beautiful woman I have ever seen, was all she said.

I asked, Are you both the same age then?

Jeanie told me, No, she is a year and three months to the day older than me.

58

SHANE

So why did she leave if you were in love with each other, I asked?

We weren't in love with each other we just had sex because we are the two best looking girls around and she didn't want to give her virginity away to just anyone, Jeanie explained. I have Justin and she didn't have that mister right in her life. She left because her family were killed.

Well, it seems to me you got going sexually at a tender age, If I would have been here I would have object strongly. But I wasn't.

Nicky was calm enough to tell Justin the problem now but still seemed to be having trouble spitting it out. Justin began to ask probing questions to try to get some of what she was so upset for.

She finally said I am so confused about my life.

Justin said, do you think you could be a little more specific?

I am afraid to love anyone because all the people I loved were take away from me and I don't know if I am willing to go though that again, Nicky explained.

Well no body can make that choice for you but, I can give you my opinion on that subject. I lost my dad for fifteen years and then got him back.

SHANE

Yes, but you all got everything back and I just get to suffer, Nick blurted.

O'yah, if you think life is cruel to you think about this, your family were taken by God but dad's are here and he can't have them because somebody else has them, Justin informed her sternly!

I never thought about knowing they are there and not being able to see them, that would drive me nuts I think Nicky said.

Jeanie looked at me and said, you're the only person other than me who has made love with Nicky.

Wrong, I never made love to Nicky, I whispered to her.

But you spent the night with her in bed and I thought from the way she acted that you had quite the sexual experience, Jean said in confusion.

Jeanie, I have been hurt a lot lately and I don't want to hurt little Nicky, I said.

Sean, I think she loves you, Jeanie said.

I looked at Jeanie for a long slow minute sizing up what I thought she meant by that, because she was a schemer and might be up to some deviltry.. I looked back to the waves that crashed on the midnight shore and thought to myself , do I really want to deal with this or do I want to rejoin the human race. I

SHANE

turn to Jean.

How could you tell, when you were having sex, I asked off the top of my head?

  Jeanie said, don't tell me you're jealous of our little sex on the beach, Would you feel better if I had sex with you?

  Jeanie did you just forget about Justin or something, I asked without looking at her?

  No, we aren't married and I do as I please until I'm married then only Justin gets this fantastic body and no other. So do you want to sleep with me, she said with conviction?

  Yes, but I don't want Justin to know. Let me ask you a question, say Justin went out and screwed a chick what would you do and how would you feel, I quipped?

Without missing a beat Jeanie said, I am sure that he has but I don't care I love him for him, not for my hold on him.

Strangely, Jeanie I would love to enjoy you but I can't, maybe in another life, but not this one. Justin is more important to me than any sex, with anyone. Even you. Moreover Jean', if Nicky really cares for me it would break her tiny little heart to think I betrayed her. Besides your just talking shit, testing me... go ahead deny it.

Jeanie only smiled.

SHANE

Back at the cabins, Justin said, is dad who your in love with?

 Nicky held her breath then admitted that I was the man of her desires.

Justin said, what if he went out and had sex with bunch of babes how would you feel?

 I want to be the only lover he needs but I would overlook it if I was number one in his life, Nicky whispered.

 Justin said you got it bad for him, don't you? Then he smiled.

 Yes! Nicky said what about you what would you do Jeanie was fooling around on you?

 Well, Justin replied, she has sex with you and I don't bitch do I.

 Nicky said, Jeanie doesn't know you know about that, as she stared at the floor out of embarrassment.

Justin lifted her chin and said, I don't blame her your the most beautiful woman on earth, besides her. Besides as long as she has been on the beach she is probably humpin dad by now.

 Nicky got up and ran as fast as she could down to the beach.

Justin smiled wryly to himself, then followed her to see what was going to happen when she found Jean and I. Nicky ran past

SHANE

when I saw her and yelled at her to stop. She turned ran up and jumped into my arms and started crying.

Jeanie said, something to Justin and they both began to smile, and then they walked away.

Sean, I want to ask you something. DO YOU LOVE ME?

　Morning came and Nicky still had not slept because she asked me if I loved her and I told her that a question like that needed some thought even though I knew that I was in love with her already I did not want to devalue the moment by saying yes when she was excited.

I said, let's you and I go for a walk shall we?

　Nicky got up without a word and went with me half afraid I was going to give her bad news.

　A mile or so down the beach from the lighthouse I stopped by a big rock and told Nicky to pop a squat. She sat in total silence. I turned to her and started to speak when she cut me off.

　If your going to blow me off just do it and let me go, don't make me suffer, she screamed!

　Nicky, shut up! I didn't answer your question last night because you were hysterical and I didn't want you to think I said yes as a nee-jerk reaction.

SHANE

Nicky, I LOVE YOU AND I WANT TO BE WITH YOU, I told her!

She looked at me a moment then started crying.

I thought, hey, what's the matter babe but I didn't say it because the ground was currently hers and she was going to have to use it sooner or later.?

Nicky looked up with tears just pouring out of her little eyes and said I was so afraid I was making a fool out of myself and you were just being nice so you would not hurt my feelings!

Sean, I know that you have had a bad go of it over the years, I want to make up for that, but I don't know how, she said through the tears.

Nicky just be with me, that's all anyone could do for me, and above all be true to yourself I don't care for phonies, I told her.

We returned to the lighthouse area where we enjoyed the food that Justin had made for us.

How's life old man, jested Justin?

Watch who your calling old pal, I can take you down and pin your ears back, I told the boy.

Right, come in and eat you both look hungry as horses, Justin said.

SHANE

Nicky said, where is Jeanie?

Justin said, she was very tired so she is still in bed.

Nicky got up then, I'll be back in a couple minutes. She walked out and made a bee-line for Jeanie's room.

Justin, what do you think about a person who cheats on their lover?

Justin looked at me then said, did you have sex with Jeanie last night dad?

What do you think happened son?

Well, I don't know, but I wouldn't blame you if you did have sex with her last night, he answered.

Justin, I asked what you thought not whether you would blame me or not.

I don't think you would ever do anything that would hurt me, that is what I think, he said.

Well son, you got me pegged all right, I said. He just smiled and began eating and I did also.

Jeanie wasn't sleeping when Nicky came in. Nicky walked over and took off her shoes and crawled into bed with Jeanie.

SHANE

Jeanie said, come in to ask a question?

Yes, actually I did, Nicky told her. Did you know that Justin knows about us? Second, I want to know if you slept with Sean!?

No, on both accounts sweetheart, I offered Sean my body and he turned me down cold, But he told me it was because he loved you and Justin too much to screw things up by having me, Jean said.

Nicky looked hard at her friend then said, Jeanie what would you have done if he had wanted your body?

I guess I would have to sleep with him, Jeanie said as she yawned.

Do you want to be with him, Nicky asked?

No Nicky, he and Justin are two of a kind and I have one already I don't need the other.

Nicky and Jeanie laid in bed holding each other talking about their plans for us in the future. Meanwhile, in the galley Justin and I talked about what we were going to do in the future for a business.

Justin said, you can't keep hiding from life forever dad, you got Nicky to think about now.

Son, I got more money than I could probably ever spend already

SHANE

so is that are you talking about?

 Dad, you have allot to give, so kick out dude, your still a young man with a nearly iron fighting style, your one of the best little men the sport has ever known, so why not teach it, he said?

 I said, I'll teach you and you can be my partner.

 I don't know, I think people will think I'm riding your coattails and I don't have what it takes to teach your style dad, he said.

 When did you start giving a damn what fools think, besides after I teach you they will be too afraid to say that to your face and who is to say what it takes to teach my way, since it is made up from all the Martial arts I have studied I told him.

 OK, it's a deal, he said as he shook my hand.

    The girls were sleeping in each others arms totally unaware that they were sleeping away the day. Justin motioned to me to come and look at the girls asleep over here. I walked over and looked in the door of Justin's room at the two sleeping beauties.

Justin said to himself, Justin is it going to bother you that our lovers make love with each other? Then he answered himself as if he were two people carrying on a conversation No, I have known for a long time that they were doing that, I don't mind.

 In the galley a phone rang and it was my friend and former training partner Bob the Bouncer. Bob wanted to know if he

67

SHANE

could come over and talk to me since he was in the general area.

Say Bob, what would you do if I said no, I asked?

 I would have gone home, Bob answered.

 I said, Come over then dude.

  When Bobby arrived an hour later I woke Nicky, who was giving me that I'm to tired to get up routine. She and Jeanie finally got up and ate some food then dressed themselves. Bob drove up in a new car and got out in new cloths, walked around like he was in a fashion show.

Bob said, what do ya think of m'new shit?

Nice digs ol' buddy, I said.

Yeah, but not as nice as her, Bob said!

 I turned to see Jeanie standing in the door of her room smiling at us.

 Wow, there's two of them, you dog your holding out on me man, Bob asked!

 Nicky walked up to me and kissed my neck, then wrapped her arms around me and said love ya.

 Bob must have realized that Nicky was unavailable because he

68

SHANE

made a line for Jeanie. Bob reached out to put his hand on Jeanie's hip when he came face up on Justin.

She's with me Bob, said Justin!

Hell, I didn't know Justin. Sorry man didn't mean t'get yer dander up.

Back to biz I guess, I came here to see if your going to come back and compete for your title? If you are I'll train ya bud, he said then took a deep breath as if it was hard to say.

It would appear your doing just fine for your self now Bobber.

I came into some inheritance, Bob explained.

Nicky said, are you going to go Sean? Nicky's face was very serious all of a sudden. What are you going to do with me if you decide to go?

TAKE YOU WITH, what the hell did you think, I asked?

Nicky said, I don't know that is why I ask. You could always be my girl if Sean dumps ya babe, said Bob.

Justin said, shut up you ass.

I said, Do you want to go Nicky?

Where you go I go. I would follow you anywhere, I love you Sean,

69

SHANE

Nicky said.

Jeanie and Justin ran Bob into the galley for some Java and Bob followed them because it appeared that I was going to be engaged elsewhere for at least a little while.

I carried Nicky to the beach and said, what would you like to do, you're my life now, I told her?

That night I took Nicky to a nice little restaurant and wined and dined her as sweat as I could without being silly which I probably was. We had Fettuccini Alfredo ala herb (who was the cook, he liked Nicky) and root beer shakes. I asked Nicky if she was having a good time honey? She told me that she was and , is it always going to be like this?

I told her I hope so baby, but your going to have humor me sometimes if we're going to have loads of good times. We took a fairy across the bay to see what was over there, just enjoying doing things together.

We had just found out how deep our love was for each other without actually asking the question. The boat rocked as the waves caressed its side rolling it around like a cat would a ball of yarn.

Nicky said the movement of the boat tickled her tummy.

Back at the lighthouse Justin was getting tired of the way Bob was slobbering over his women, yet Jean seemed to enjoy the

SHANE

attention that she was getting. The phone rang and Justin answered it.

The voice said is Sean there?

Justin asked, who is calling?

So, he is there huh! The phone went dead.

Bob turned from the window he was looking out and said, Justin get your tail over here quick (in a calm tone). Who are they bud?

No idea bob, let's find out, Justin said as he peered out the window.

Jeanie pulled out her gun and found a good position to fight from if things turned ugly.

Bob took off his jacket and looked at Justin and said let's rock man.

Justin slapped him a five and said right!

There were six men standing outside dressed alike with the same look on there face. They all looked like Harry Christaners on acid and they moved like a snake all at once in a uniformed pattern As if they were attached to one another.

One of them stepped up to Bob and said Sean you'll come with

SHANE

me.

   Sorry to disappoint you dick, but I'm not Sean, said Bob.

   Is he then, pointing at Justin, asked the bald man?

   No, he is not bud and that's strike two care to swing again, Bob
said, Say pal, what do you want my friend for anyway?

The strange man let the question slide without a change of
expression and said, then you will tell us where he is.

Fat chance of that, said Justin as he finished rolling up his
sleeves.

   The man rejoined the other five men and they all pulled short
shafts from their long coats in unison.

   Then the man who spoke before said we will force you to tell us
then boy.

All six of the men moved in a well-rehearsed manner together.

   Looked at that Justin, trained dogs.

   Three of the strangers engaged Bob and the others took on
Justin.

The men who attacked Bob underestimated him and he grabbed
one of them and broke his neck. The other two jumped back in

72

SHANE

shear surprise at Bob's skill and speed.

Justin went on the attack, but one of the men's staffs touched his arm and he nearly passed out from it. The three men leapt forth to subdue Justin, but he had already recovered and was laying possum. As they approached he let them come in until he could easily reach them all. The first man held out his staff to touch Justin again, then the others did as the first man had done. Justin caught them so off guard that he knocked all three down at once. He then kicked their weapons away and beat them as hard as he could without killing them. Bob had no problem with his opponents, subduing them without any great effort.. After all the goons were tied up they decided to question them about their motives.

A very large robed person appeared and said that's enough!

Bob said, who are you and what do you want pal?

The large darkly clad figure did not reply, instead he waved his hand and the five men were no longer tied up and even more curious the guy Bob killed was getting up and going over to the large figure.

Bob turned to Justin and said, I think were in trouble bud.

SHANE

SHANE

CHAPTER THREE: THE QUEST. . . .

   The large person motioned to the men that Justin and Bob had
fought to get behind and sit upon the ground.

   At just that moment Justin nudged Bob and said all of those
guys look exactly alike.

   Bob looked and said, yeah your right now if I could only get my
shorts out of my throat I could probably come up with a plan.
   However, before Bob could get his briefs out of his throat,
the large figure spoke.

   The large figure took a step forth and Bob got into a fighting
stance.

   Justin put his hand on Bob's arm and said, I think we are out of
our league with a guy who brings dead guys to life Bobby.

Bob stood up straight and said, right man.

The figure reached up and pulled back it's hood. The face below
was weathered and gaunt yet strangely hansom. I did not mean
for all of this unpleasantness to be imposed on you, I simply
sent these men to find Sean Savage.

   Justin said, what do you want with him.

SHANE

   The overly large man took yet another step forth and said I have done him a great injustice and I want to make right the wrong done.

Bob said how do we know we can trust you, after all you brought a dead guy to life.

   The strange man said first my name is Goth. I am keeper of the gates of the time. What I want Sean for is the master key that I alone was entrusted was taken from the corridor of lasting shadows.

Justin asked what happened to the key, what the hell do you want with my dad?

   Jeanie who had watched the whole affair came out of the galley and said if he is sincere then we should sit down and talk in the galley.

   Meanwhile Nicky and I were just reaching the end of the fairy ride. The evening was pleasant, a breeze was blowing in from the ocean and the air was crisp.

   Nicky looked at me and said you look strange all of the sudden what the matter with you.

I said, there is something wrong with my son.

   Nicky said, how do you know?

SHANE

I just have the feeling that he's in danger, I said.

She said, do you want to call to see what's up?

Yeah, I do, I said.

So, we went and found a phone booth to call Justin. I fished around in my pockets for a quarter but I didn't have one so asked Nicky for one.

Nicky said, let me see.

Before she could reach into her pocket, I said, let me look for it.

My hand went in her pocket and fished around.

Nicky started giggling and said, that's not a quarter.

I laughed while pulling my hand from her pocket, but this is, I said.

I dialed the number for Justin's room and let it ring.

Justin finally answered the phone.

Justin is that you, I asked?
  Yeah, it's me, who's this, he inquired?

Who the hell do you think it is, I demanded?

SHANE

I don't know, so tell me because I don't have time for stupid games.

I growled into the phone by mistake.

Justin said, You sound just like me, it's dad, hey dad, there's a weird guy here who says his name is Goth.

There was a long period of dead silence, then I said no matter what you do don't let him get away.

Justin asked, do you know this guy?

Kind of, I'll explain later.

OK dad, I'll see you when you get here.

Nicky said, what's up?

I said I'll explain on the way home. We jumped in the truck and hit the highway. As I explained what was going on to Nicky in the best details I could muster, she sat silently.

We reached the light house and Jeanie was there to greet us.

Jeanie said, wait till I tell you what's been going on.

Nicky cut Jeanie off in mid-sentence by saying never mind that stuff, just listen to what I got to say.

78

SHANE

At that very moment Goth came out and said so I finally get to meet you.

   You speak as if you've know me for a long while, why is that, I asked?

   You were pulled into one of the gates of time to be a diversion for someone who wanted to take the Key Of Time, Goth explained.

 Why tell me about it, what can I do, I am only one man, I asked?

   You know what the entity who took the key looks like, said Goth.

   I said, how do you figure?

He is the one who told you how to get back to this time period.

OK, but what do you want from me anyway, I asked?

   You must get the key back for me, said Goth.
   Justin spoke up, why do you need us if you can bring the dead to life?

   I turned to him and asked, what's that son?

   Bob said, I killed one of those jokers and laughing boy brought'em back to life.

79

SHANE

Goth spoke, I can't bring anything to life nor kill anyone, yet I do posses certain
abilities that you might think grand.

Bob said then you go get this bastard and leave Sean be.

I wish I could, but I can't, because I don't actually enter any time period.

Nicky said, you're here now.

I said, he's not really here, he's a hologram, Goth what can I do to help you retrieve the key?

Sean, I have a smaller version of the Key Of Time for you to use to find the main key and return it. This key (at that moment he pulled a key from his robe) is the Key Of Destiny, it has three brother's Truth, Justice and Hope, Goth explained.

Goth why did you choose the Key Of Destiny for me, I asked him?
The answer to that question will be revealed to you in time but for now I'll tell you that the other three keys will not be standing idle in this matter, Goth told me.

Bob, suddenly blurted out why can't one of these clowns do it instead of my buddy?

Goth said, come here a moment Robert.

SHANE

Bob walked over to Goth and he listened to the giant man for
a moment.

   Justin said I wonder what he is saying to Bob?

Goth had his mammoth hand on Bob's shoulder and Bob didn't
seem
to mind. Bob turned and faced us smiled then waved and he
Disappeared. We all must have looked a bit startled because

   Goth said he is fine, he has chosen to take a task in this
matter. Sean will you come with me to retrieve the key of which
I have spoke?

Yes, but not until the morning.

   Silence blanketed the land and tears ran down my chest. Nicky
was not even still awake, yet still the tears fell. I was strangely
calm about the whole spiel and at the same time I was horrified
at the prospect of never seeing Nicky again. I did not want to
sleep, I wanted to spend my last night with
this love I had been lucky enough to find.

   A few hours before dawn a knock at my door came. I got
up and answered it.

   Justin said, get dressed we need to talk.

We walked only out of the lighthouse courtyard when Justin

SHANE

turned and said, don't go dad, I don't trust Goth.

Son if I don't go there might be no here to stay at soon, was my answer.

   Justin just stood there knowing I had been brutally honest with him, but could not help the way he felt. I went back, and took off my clothes and woke Nicky.

   She Woke with a start, then said is it time now?

   No, I just thought I should make love with you in case. . . .

   In case you never come back, said Nicky!!!

Yeah, that's it baby, I admitted.

 We spent the rest of the predawn hours loving each other as well as we knew how.

    Goth was there when the sun came up, it is time Sean to leave, he said.

   I turned to Justin, Jeanie and Nicky and said, I have no intention of saying g'bye to any of you so don't you say it either.

Goth touched my arm and I was gone. Traveling through plains of reality was kindofa hoot, it felt like falling through feathers but didn't tickle. I thought that when you traveled through time it was supposed to an instant transfer, but this was taking a while

SHANE

and it gave me time to think. I had just found a love,
lost a love. Found a son and a place to belong again and lost
both of them.

I thought that there was a certain irony in the fact that I was the
one who was needed to fix up the damage, when my own life was
a jigsaw puzzle. I thought It couldn't get any worse, but I was
wrong!

   When I stopped moving in and out of the recesses of reality
I was in front of a monument of a size, that was so large I could
not see the top of it.

 "Come in Sean I have been waiting for your arrival for what
seems even to me like an eternity, said a vibrating voice."

Who said that, I shouted?

 Come and see boy, said the same great noisy voice.

 I walked in to the huge structure carefully watching for
anything unusual which was crazy since everything here was
unusual. The hallway I was walking down was made of some
metal I don't think I ever seen before. The hallway took a turn
down and to my left, so I just kept following it down. A great
room laid ahead I could tell, and at that moment I felt scared and
excited at the same time.

 Welcome Sean Savage, I have been waiting for you, said
the giant figure in the middle of the room.

83

SHANE

My God, I said as I focused on the man of more than forty feet tall sitting in a chair that was more than likely made of diamond.

A great sight am I not, he said?

Yes you are, I said in a gasp.

Welcome my son, you are very brave to come here, he said.

How's that, when you invited me here, I asked.

I am not Goth young man, he said.

Then who are you, I inquired?

I am the one you must attend for a time to see if you be worthy to hold the Key of Destiny, he said.

This is bullshit, get your act together or I'm out of here, I growled at the giant in the husky boy clothing!

You are quite the livewire are you not, said the giant.

Okay, we'll do this your way son, I will give you three tasks and if you complete them with out fail then I will entrust the key to you. Does this meet with your approval Sean.

WHEN I finish the tasks, Fine with me, I said.   What are the tasks?

84

SHANE

The giant said, it will only give you one at time.

First, you must find my name.

How am I supposed to do that, I heatedly asked.

That as you say is your problem, the giant said as he began to laugh at my plight.

Alright is there a place where you want me to start, I asked?

He raised his massive arm and identified the way I was to take, then he looked at me and said if you survive this you will be the first my son.

The first task or all of them, I said?

The first... good luck son, he said with a serious face.

I thought to myself what am I doing here, what is here? I don't trust that guy, he was much to happy when he said I would be the first one to succeed, who tried this before me, and what happened to him? I look for the arch that the big man pointed at and saw it in the corner so I walked over to it and surveyed the damn thing for a moment before taking that first step. However, if I was going to finish this mess I would have to take that step. To enter the unknown for Nicky, for the life I had, I took the step forward...

SHANE

I found myself in a land of mostly smoke with little eerie
sounds all around. I paused for a moment to reflect on the hint
that the giant gave me, no matter how obscure it may have been,
and I made an educated guess that the sounds were danger so I
was on guard after that. My guess turned out to be a good one,
because not long after I paused I met my first obstacle. It was a
honest to goodness nightmare right out of hell and it seen me
coming so there was no going back. I started to run like hell, but
the nightmare was gaining , so I said the hell with this and
stopped and turned on my nemesis.

The creature from what I could tell seemed to be half human
and half bat and it was sporting a very bad attitude. It rushed me
and I saw that it had an equally strong body to go with it's
attitude.

When the creature saw that I was not going to run for it, it
stopped, came to a soft landing on a huge rock, folded his mighty
wings for a moment, leaned forward far enough to lick me.
Closed one eye and looked hard at me with the other open eye
and said, are you not going to run from me like the rest who
came before you.

I am not, I said with courage.

Neither were they in the beginning, too afraid I should think, but
you are a very curious little one indeed, he said smiling through
great razor sharp ivory tusks.

Well what now gruesome, I asked as I stood there shaking,

86

SHANE

trying to look tough and not pee my pants?

 I am not sure, all the others have ran for their pitiful lives yet you do not, he bellowed. I couldn't persuade you to run for it could I little snack could I, he chuckled?

 Hell no, I said strongly leaning toward him this time.

 Didn't think so, he said smiling at me.

 Then you must give me something for making your game more of a challenge, I offered as a suggestion.

 The creature regarded me for a moment, then smiled again and said what do you ask of me small one?

I shall only ask for one thing and then may I leave in peace, unharmed and un-followed for future ambush?

 Yes, you have made this day special for me. ASK, he roared!

 What is the name of the giant who lives just beyond here, I inquired?

 The man-bat drew back so swiftly that I nearly fell down from the wind.

 Why do you need this information little one, he asked looking at me very carefully for the answer in my body language if my tongue lied?

SHANE

The giant has charged me with the task of learning his name, I told him.

I can't tell you, said the beast.

Are you then not going to honor your word, I scolded?

Mine, is the word of a titan boy and is therefore unbreakable, he roared in disgust.

Then why won't you tell me what I need to know, I politely asked?

Because, little friend I do not know myself or I would banish that evil bastard personally, he said with great pride as he flexed his titanic muscles. He is the reason I am in the shaded hades, I hate him and wish to crush the life from him and eat what remains of him.

I drew very near the great man-bat, because I was no longer in fear for my life and said, please explain, as we are friends you must share your thoughts with me.

The beast smiled and said, your as smart as you are brave little friend.

Come, he said then turned and took wing, it was like a 747 taking off, so I had to hold my ears so they would not bust from the loud sound..

SHANE

 I followed the beast who would more than likely kill me
and dine on my intestines that very evening. However, if he was
going to let me have it there wasn't anything I could do to save
myself so I just followed.

 Finally the man-bat alighted on the top of a stone. As I
approached I saw that their was a doorway behind where we
were.

 Listen carefully friend, said the creature, the giant can be
controlled by saying his name in reverse or rhyme. Never forget
this, never! Behind us is the way to the land of Bnurr, home of a
wise old troll who once came to me for a favor, he can help you I
am sure.

 I started out through the door and the beast caught me by the
arm and said I still owe you something and it must be paid.

 I looked into his picture window eyes, thought for a moment,
then don't kill for sport anymore, I said, you don't seem to be
blood thirsty, just bored.

 Done, said the man-bat, but you must come back and talk with
me again.

 I said, what are you called?

 Once a long time ago I knew the answer to that but no more.

SHANE

Then I shall call you Windrider or Rider for short, I said to him with a smile.

I see no fault in that grand name, I should think it will suit me well. What are you called my tiny brave friend?

Sean, I said.

Once you go thru the portal I will be alone and trapped again, and it has been a abominable long time with no voice but my own. Come back Sean, don't subject me to this misty hell forever more. Rider said in a bellowing low tone that could crush stone.

If I can in life or death release you from this place I will , you have my word, I will return or die trying, I said earnestly.

The once terrifying titan, looked at me with barrel sized tears at the ready in his massive eyes. I had touched his giant heart somehow and he believed in me.

You must be a king in your world to speak such powerful words, I will serve you willingly if you can get me out of here. Say farewell brave one before I beg you not to leave and embarrass myself.

I touched the titans powerful shoulder, turned on a heel and stepped thru the gateway.

I left Rider and began looking for a troll. I had never seen a troll except in a storybook, so I didn't know when I would come across one. I walked for miles and then I just stop and sat

90

SHANE

because I was so tired and had not eaten in what seemed to me
to be days. I thought to myself that I had been lucky with my
new found ally Windrider, however how long am I going to be able
to function on dumb luck. I got back to my feet and started
walking. The land I was in now was not like the one I had left,
this place was bright and sunny. Night fell hard and I was lost
and I was starving to death.

 Damn, if I don't find this dude soon I'll starve to death for God's
sake, I said out loud.

"Is that right boy", said a voice in the dark to my immediate right.

I nearly defecated.

 Who's there, I asked thinking I don't need anymore surprises?

 Does it matter said the voice, then a thing that looked like an
apple fell towards
me.

I caught it, I said thanks looking around like a dog trying to catch
his tail.

 No biggy son, said the voice in the dark.

 Why don't you come into the light so I can see you, I asked?

 I will after you eat your food, it said.

SHANE

   I ate the fruit eagerly and wiped my face with the back of my hand.

   I am done come out now, I said.

   The trees I was sitting by bent sideways as the person came forth. I thought great and you asked for this, so your to blame if this turns ugly. It did suddenly!

   Holly cow I said when I focused on my host, he was not human at all!. If I wasn't sitting down I would have fallen at the sight of my host.

   Are you afraid little man, said my host?

   Well, let me see if you had wanted to kill me I would already be toast I said.

What is toast, said the giant thing before me?

   It is bread that has been toasted over a flame or heat, I explained.

   This toast sounds good to me said the thing.

   It was every bit twice as big as the giant man who sent me here, however it was blue-green in color and had eyes that were so red that they seemed to be endless solid rubies. Further, it had four arms that were fortified with heavy muscles and two massive powerful legs to support the giant. This guy's muscles

SHANE

could put Arnold to shame as a girly-man.

 I am Ger and as you might have noticed I'm not quite human, he said.

 Are you a troll, I asked?

 No, I am a hidden giant forest titan. I protect this forest from the Firewitchs, demons and trolls, he told me.

Ger can you tell me where to find Bnurr the troll, I asked?

Ger jumped to his feet and said are you his friend, he needled?

 If I were would I ask you where the hell he is at, I blurted.

 Then why do you seek that one, he inquired?

 Windrider told me that Bnurr could help me find the name of the giant who is at the gateway to this plane.

 Windrider, do you mean the man-bat titan in the land of shadows, he asked?

 Yes, he is my friend, I said.

 Funny I would think that he should fancy you a sup, Ger said.

 Well, he did first, but I showed him that I was better to talk with than eat.

SHANE

Ger sat and listened to my tale of how the Key of Time chose
me to hold it and return it to it rightful owner.

I began to shiver from the intense cold in the night and Ger said
lord, what's wrong with me I know that humans need heat at
night for warmth.

At that he dug a hole in the ground away from the trees
and spit fire into it.

Wow, I didn't know that you could breath fire Ger, I said.

I don't breath it little friend, I spit it, he corrected me.
All Titans can do this.

Is the gate giant a titan Ger, I asked him while he worked?

Yes, and he is going to die some day by my own hands for his
crimes, said Ger and his eyes began to glow.

If you want him dead why just go and kill him, I asked?

I have two reasons my friend, if I leave to kill the giant of the
gate the Firewitchs will burn down my forests, second that clever
son of a bitch at the gateway used his powers to prevent one
titan to cross over another titans lands, or Rider and I would
still be together and gateboy would be …. TOAST!

It was obvious to me I must fix it so my titan friends could free

94

SHANE

themselves from the land barriers.

Ger, I can help you if I find Bnurr, I said.
  Ok I will help you find him tomorrow, he told me.

  It is tomorrow now we talked all night Ger, and thanks for keeping me warm last night, I said.

  Morning in this world was like the first day that God created the earth, it was fresh, teaming with life and hope of something better, funny but I knew this from just seeing it, Ger was one with the vegetation so he could feel the majesty of it all. We left when the sun was up.

  The journey went fast because I sat upon the great shoulder of Ger as he ran. Miles went by so fast that I don't think I could travel this far in a year. We reached the castle of Bnurr the troll at dusk that night.

  I asked Ger how far we had traveled and he smiled and said a life time Sean. The two of us walked up to the door and Ger motioned to me that I should knock. The moment my knuckles touched the door it opened and Bnurr the troll stood before me glaring at Ger.

  Bnurr, I have come.

  "Silence human", said the troll. Why are you here Ger, asked Bnurr?

95

SHANE

I have brought the Sean to ask you a question old enemy, he said.

Bnurr did not look as though he believed Ger but he didn't say it instead he turned to me and said what do you want.

I was pretty damn mad at this point so I started to look Bnurr, who's name means dung up and down. He was three times my size and ten times my weight at least, he had a pointy nose, grayish skin, long nail and a set of very bad manners, much like Ebenezer Scrooge.

I demand the name of the gate giant, I yelled in the trolls face while I continued to looked up at him in disgust.

Bnurr showed his teeth and reached out to hit me, but I raise my right hand which held the Key of Destiny and blasted Bnurr across his own courtyard with a red flash of light. I was followed by Ger walked in the courtyard up to Bnurr who laid on his back with smoke rising off his chest where I had blasted him.

Listen up asshole Windrider told me that you knew the name of the gate giant and I want it!

Who is this Windrider, he asked as he got up off his duff?

The Man-bat said Ger.

Bnurr laugh, the bat would eat you not help you puny human.

SHANE

If I am so puny why are you on your back with smoke coming from your chest, I asked?

After a long pause and a thoughtful look at me, Bnurr said true enough.

Then he got to his feet and grabbed my wrist and said The Key, how did you get this little man? Before I could answer he ripped the key out of my hand.

Let us see how you defend yourself without the key boy, the troll said?

At that he tipped the long heavily jeweled staff in my direction, and lightning leapt from the big ruby on the end and hit me. I fell back a few steps, gritted my teeth and stomped hard on the ground. It shook so hard that Bnurr and Ger both fell down. I calmly walked over to the troll and held out a hand, but didn't utter a single word, because I didn't think it would help any. Ger was rolling on the ground laughing his heart out. Bnurr was visibly angered at his display.

What in Hades is so funny, asked the troll?

You can't take his power away by taking the key, you see he doesn't have the key, he is the Key of Destiny you old fool every since he touch it, Ger said as tears of joy fell from his huge eyes.

They both looked at me.

SHANE

Goth gave me the key, because the Key of Destiny chose me to hold it, I explained.

Bnurr bowed gracefully, then said "You who are Destiny may ask anything".

I wish to know the name of the giant, I asked?.

Bnurr laughed at me, then he composed himself and said young Lord Destiny you already have the means to help yourself.

I said the key would tell me then?

No, but his brother key Truth would do anything for you. Bnurr's face grew suddenly solemn with concern, the gate giant was fooled by Truth to protect you from him because you didn't realize until you used your powers against me that you had any.

Does my powers come from the key I hold friend troll I asked?

No, lord they come from within you from your soul.

I also noticed that you had a great power within you when you entered my forest Lord Destiny, so I went to see if you were true or evil said Ger.

What would you do if I were evil, I inquired?

Ger said, I would have battled you for I am the strongest force in this land and none dare challenge me here.

SHANE

You would have lost if we warred Ger, I suddenly knew to say.

Yes, Sean but I would have trapped you here on my plane forever before I fell to you as we all are unable to leave our own lands to go to next, the titan said.

Dear gentle Ger you are mistake about being able to trap me here, Lord Truth has educated me telepathically in this matter. Since I have accepted the mantel of Destiny I may move from one plane to the next uninhibited by anything, I explained as the knowledge came to me in my mind, from a familiar source yet one I could not place.

The next moment Ger said my forest is in danger from the Firewitchs and I am to far away to save them this time, at he roared and shook his four fists at the sky.

Be still Ger I said. I raised my hand and said "Windrider come forth and serve me now I have need of you". The air around the three of us burst into flames and Windrider sprang forth like the phoenix of legend.

"FREE"!! I AM FREE, at last free to soar in the light again.

Bnurr got down on his knees and hid his face in the dirt so nobody could see that he was showing emotion, because trolls are not supposed to have any. It was then that I noticed that Rider was red in color, in fact he was the color of Ger's eyes. Ger and Rider hug each other as they are best friends.

SHANE

Bnurr are you a titan as they are I said?

No, I am but a troll wizard in your service my lord, he answered.

Enough, we have to save the forests of Ger, I ordered.

Windrider said what would you ask of me Sean?

Ger then told Rider that I am The Key Master of Destiny.

Rider's giant head ripped around to regard me. Windrider dropped down on a Mack truck sized knee and said we titans have always been servants of the key masters so charge me little man and I will do.

I need your powerful wings to carry me to the forests of Ger to deal with the Firewitchs, I told him.

Climb on behind my ears and I will bring you faster than any other, he told me.

With me securely on his massive shoulders Windrider sprang handily into the air, hovering just above Ger who he grabbed with his mighty arms saying your forest need you as well old friend.

Ger grabbed onto Rider with his upper set of arms and we took off at nearly the speed of sound with
one powerful flap of Rider's wings and the more he flapped the faster we went until hundreds of miles went by a second, then

SHANE

suddenly we were there. What had taken Ger half a day to run
we had flown in two minutes.

 The forests were burning wildly when we approached I told
Rider to drop Ger so he could nail anyone one the ground. Rider
did as I bid him. Ger hit the ground running catching six
Firewitchs totally off guard. Ger trapped them in Amber so he
could continue to fight.

 Windrider put me on the ground I said.

Once upon the ground I told Windrider to drive the winged
Firewitchs from the sky toward me.

 Rider said no flame shall remain.

 I sat on the dirt watching my titan pals fight an epic
battle. Finally the Firewitchs were making a run for it because
they were only ready to battle one titan instead of two, and
they still had not noticed me. They would come to wish that
they had, because they were running for it alright but that
was right at me. I let them get about forty yards from me then

I held up my hand and said fire and fly no more.

 One screamed it's Destiny, but it was to late all of them
plummeted into the earth below. To say they hit the ground hard
would be a gross understatement, because some of them were
completely buried by the impact of the fall. They all were alive
but some were hurt pretty bad, yet all of them looked right at me

SHANE

and shook in fear.

Despite his fear the leader of the firewitchs came forth and said Lord Destiny we are at your mercy. Please, he said we are Firewitchs and Ger is our sworn enemy so we had to burn the forests.

I listened to him and could see he was just a soldier doing his sovereign bidding, yet Ger was going wild, so my attention needed to shift for the moment, I told the Firewitchs to sit and wait.

I told Ger and Rider to watch the prisoners while I took a walk through the burn down forest to see how bad the damage really was. The fires had done their job well Ger's forest was razed and Ger himself seemed to be ill over the scene. I walked toward him to console him over the great loss he faced, but Rider stopped me by saying look Ger where ever Sean steps life in the earth is renewed. Everywhere new plants and trees were springing up into the light bringing the forest back to life.

Ger fell to his gigantic knees to examine the dirt and he said this day yonder Firewitchs shall not be punished as harshly as I had planned.

Windrider growled and asked if he could please be allowed to eat them as he is simply famished.

No, old friend I think that we shall never know peace if there is only killing and no effort to cleanse the wound their will always

102

SHANE

be war here.

The leader of the Firewitchs came forth and knelt at my feet.

What will you do with us Lord Destiny, he asked?

In the words of a great old spaceman take me to your leader, I said almost laughing.

The witch said you want me to take you to our king?

That is exactly what I want you to do Pyro, I told him.

Who is this Pyro my lord asked the Firewitchs?

That is what I am going to call you bravest of the Firewitchs, I said to him, which brought a smile.

The journey to the palace of the king of the Firewitchs took two days. There was a huge army waiting for me and my comrades when we arrived. A smartly dressed winged soldier approach and said you have no right to be here, leave at once or be killed.

He was about to turn to leave when he spotted Pyro behind me. The guard left anyway.

SHANE

SHANE

CHAPTER- 4 - THE KING OF FIRE.

The army of Firewitchs attack with impunity. I motioned to Windrider to rule the sky and he did just that, although there were thousands of them they were no match for his horrible titan powers. Ger blasted witches out of the sky with his own fire like a great artillery battery.

I stood by and let the battle progress for rider's sake since he had been trap for so long alone.   There was no doubt that I had made the right decision about not slaying our captive Firewitchs, but I did so to prevent a war and now we were knee deep in that very thing.

The tide of battle turned toward me and for the first time I felt as if I had to be careful not to use to much force against the unsuspecting foe. I cleared my mind and thought if I wear to defeat the wing terror without killing I better act quick.

The voice of Truth was once again telepathically in my head telling me that Firewitchs can not take the cold.

As the winged death approach me, I wondered if I was invulnerable to harm as a key master.   However, I decided not to test it at present, I paused to look at how beautiful the sky was because of the fire from the titans which was one color and the fire from the witches was another.   The approaching Firewitchs

SHANE

return my attention back to the battle.

  I said to them guard yourselves witches I am no helpless human, they didn't listen. I raised my left hand to heaven and call to God for mercy to any who were about to be sent his way and then my hand turned bright blue like the deep sea and ice and sleet, snow and hail erupted from the air just beyond my finger tips. The shear force of the ice killed half of there numbers instantly. Further the sleet and snow blinded and drove the rest of the Firewitchs from the sky. Once on the ground the hail pounded them in to the ground and those who survived were very docile.

  The titans had all who were alive all rounded up by the time the messenger from the Fire king arrived. Ger nearly trampled her because she was so small, in fact she was my size and very pretty.

  She walked right up to me and said who are you to have two titans and a magic key in your command.

  He is the living Lord of Destiny, said Pyro.

  She turned and said that's bullshit the Key Masters are not human, for no man has the wisdom or purity to wield the power of the Keys. Then she turned and said are you a demon in disguise?

No, I am a man and a Key, I said.

106

SHANE

Windrider said, who are you to question our lord, wretch?

I am the princess of the sky, daughter of the Fire king.

Well, Lodi da baby girl said Rider.

I am Windrider titan of the sky and have no equal there, so I hope your not to insulted if I don't grovel at your tiny feet little snack he said smiling through missile sized, razor sharp teeth.

Worry not little Sky, Rider won't sup on you unless I say it is well. Rider looked disappointed, but Ger reached down and grabbed the girl in his second right hand and was about to crush her for what her father was guilty for.

I said no, she is not to be harmed, but he still proceeded so I through lightning from all ten fingers at him and not one finger failed it's mark.

Ger was picked up by the mighty blast and thrown hundred yards away landing on his side. I ran over to where he laid and pulled the girl from his grip.

Rider flew up behind me and said that Ger just got carried away and to be forgiving of his anger.

Ger achieved his feet looking down on me, then knelt and said I ask for you to forget this, for I forgot none may escape Destiny.

Are you well, I mean your not hurt are ya Ger?

SHANE

No, I am well he said. It will take a great deal more than a little shock to injure me.

I looked at him and made a mental note of just how Oh MY GOD powerful he obviously must be.

The girl said you are truly Lord Destiny.

Rider asked has your temper always been so violent little lord?

I'm afraid so, I admitted.

Let's raze the castle said Ger, it is the least the king should get.

I looked at Rider and he inclined his head in a way that meant it was just. So I looked a Ger and nodded.

Ger razed the castle in record time finding that most of it's main forces had been beaten earlier outside the castle. However, Ger did not find the King of Fire in the castle. Sky knew he was there I thought but I knew that she would not betray her father, so I grabbed her by her throat in the throne room and ripped her clothing off her body yelling that if the king did not show up soon she would play the role of courtesan to me and others until she was dead.

He sprang forth and said release my daughter villain or die badly, but he did not notice that the pillars he stood next to were

SHANE

Ger's leg, until they moved.

  The Firewitchs that were following me into the throne room were laughing at their own king, which pissed him off.

  I turned to Sky said I was sorry I had to do that, but she didn't seem to mind.

  I waved my hand over her and her cloths were the way they were before I ripped them, Sky smiled at me.

  Ger had the king of the Firewitchs tightly held in all four arms to make sure that he wasn't going anywhere. Pyro stepped forward and explained what was going on briefly to his lord and at the end he explained who I was.

  The king regarded me for a time, then exclaimed you won't succeed little fool. Because without your key your another puny worm.

  I removed the Key of Destiny from the pouch I had it in and through it to the Fire king, you mean that key pal?

  He laugh, pointed the key at me and of-course nothing happened.

The king said this is not the real key! Once again everybody laughed at him.

  Windrider landed on the floor near me, he bent over and looked

SHANE

the Fire king in the eye saying you don't know as much as you thought do ya?

 Ger spoke, Sean doesn't carry the Key of Destiny he is the Key of Destiny.

 Further, we came here to bring peace to this land and the next the day went well after the king surrendered his castle to Ger because it was Ger's home that had been ravaged by fire, although it was going to grow back quickly. The king and Ger and signed a treaty of peace and that is what we had.

Sky came to me and sat at my feet placing her hands over mine.

 She looked deep into my eyes and asked if I was spoken for or if I had someone back in my world?

 I have someone back in my world but I will more than likely never see her again, I told her.

 Is she very beautiful lord, Sky asked?

 Yes, she is the most beautiful woman inside and out, I said reflecting deep into my own heart..

 What do you mean inside and out, Sky asked me?

 She is very pretty to look at, has a great body and on the inside she is loving, generous, understanding an all around best bet, I explained.

110

SHANE

What is her name, Sky asked?

Nicky.

Do you love her?

I answered, Yes, more than words could express Sky.

I asked Sky, do you have someone?

No, but I wish I did so I wasn't so lonely, was her answer.

Come with me child, I said taking her by the hand and walking across the room.

Sky was no child, but a lovely young woman with a body nearly as nice as Nicky's.

I walked right up to Pyro and said Sky I have seen the way Master Pyro has looked at you with affection in his eyes but never dared to express his heart's desire to you.

Pyro who is as young and handsome as Sky is beautiful said nothing and looked down at his feet being unable to look at Sky so close to him.

Firewitchs are at-least as tall as a NBA center, slim and powerfully built, with beautiful white snowy wings on their backs. They get their name from the ability to produce and shoot fire

111

SHANE

from their finger tips. Pyro and Sky were more handsome then most.

Sky put her hand on Pyro's cheek and said look in to my eyes Pyro.

Pyro did and Sky began to cry silent tears because she could see the love in his eyes for her.

How long have you loved me Pyro, she demanded as her heart began to burn for him?

Forever, Princess was his answer, but I had no name therefore no worth so I could say nothing as a nameless soldier.

Sky turned to me and said why did you give him a name?

I held up my hand and asked for a few moments to say something. The partiers gave me silence to speak.

I said come here Pyro. He came to stand beside me though he was twice my stature. I said this man showed himself to be a great leader when I captured him and his comrades by asking for mercy for them with no concern for his own life. Therefore I gave him a powerful name fit for a prince, because he is a prince among men.

The king stepped forth and said since I have no son I proclaim that Pyro shall be know as prince of the Fire Kingdom.

SHANE

Pyro shook the kings hand and said I am a man of few words but I would say of few important ones now. I would like it very much if I could be given the honor of asking Sky to be my wife.

   The king stood there not knowing what to say but Sky jumped into Pyro's arms and said Yes a thousand times yes!

The crowd cheered and so did the surprised king who had not known laughter in the Fire Kingdom in a hundred years.

   I sat looking at the sky in a window while the celebration ensued behind me. I was being watched by two concerned titan friends and a Fire king who did not understand how I could be so unhappy with all the power I could wield.

   Ger explained the horrible task I was trying to perform for the good of all in the universe.

The king said I shall say to him that all I have is at his serve for asking.

   Windrider said that's a nice gesture but do it in the morning ok.

   They agreed and left him to watch over me.

   I cleared my mind and called out for Truth, Justice, and Hope my bother Keys to be visions in front of me so I could talk with them. Truth appeared instantly and I knew him.

   Bobby, is that you pal?

SHANE

   The hazy image before me smiled and said yes old friend it is I
but I am very different than I was before. I am no longer subject
to anger or jealousy anymore.

Yes, I said, I see the truth of it.

   Truth said remember when Goth placed his hand on my should
and I was gone?

   Yeh, I remember thinking that you were dead or worse.

   Well old friend the Bobby you knew is gone forever but all of his
memories still remain.

Truth where are our brothers, I asked?

   Justice is on his way but has not gotten use to using his
abilities yet. He is here now though.

Justin, is that you?

   Yes, strange as it may seem I was the best choice for this key.

   Do you have news of Hope, Justice, I asked?

   I know not of Hope, father or brother or what ever.

Truth said, even I do not know, Destiny.

SHANE

Where are you two at, I said?

He who would be the living instrument of truth is near the hand of God Sean, because the truth is with Jesus.

You have come a long way Bob, from bad boy to hobnobbing with God, not bad, I said.

How about you Justin, I asked him?

I am nowhere and everywhere at the same time, it is very hard to explain dad.

Well where is your body son?

My body is in a castle on top of
the asteroid that circles the sun, Justin said.

What kind of abilities do you each have, I asked them?

Truth said, I know everything on demand and can force truth out into the open by what ever means necessary.

You mean the harder the truth is to get the stronger your abilities get to compensate.

Yes, that is an accurate view, Bob said.

Justice said, I can do what ever I have to make sure Justice is served.

SHANE

Truth said, Justice can kill and so can you but I cannot.

However, I can see the future and you can't.

I said you both know where I am, but it is obvious to me that you two plus Hope are to serve me as I see fit.

Truth do you think I am correct?

I see the truth of it, all must face and serve Destiny in their own way and time.

We must find out what has befallen Brother Hope my fellow keys.

What Destiny seeks is what is, said truth, I must leave you now Sean be well and I am always with you. At that he was gone.

Tell me Justice have I done the right thing here in the land of sunshine?

You have shown yourself be worthy of leading the Keys of the Universe, and are very just in your dealing with the people showing great wisdom.

Justice bid me goodbye and disappeared. Ger had watched me all night and observed my conversation with the of keys about further plans I was mulling over in my mind.

I see the wheels turning in your head friend, said Ger.

116

SHANE

I have a great many thoughts that acquire attention, so I have not slept.

You have not slept in all the time you've been here, said Ger.

Your mind and soul are nearly omnipotent but your body is still human Sean, advised Ger with conviction.

I promised to rest when I had my plan complete, but Ger said no, now.

I had to smile because he was right I was exhausted beyond words and in badly need of rest. I curled up on a quilt and slept.

The folks of the mighty Fire Kingdom had taken to me and liked this peace that they newly enjoyed. However, the demon horde that traveled around the land razing everything were near by and demanded lodging of their old allies. Pyro newly crowned prince asked the king if he may turn them away for they only had a shaky alliance at best in the past.

The king said, Pyro my son who is to be king some day and marry Sky, you may tell those no good sons-a-bitches to kiss my fat ass with their stinking demands. Pyro had to smile at the kings witticism in the face of certain war if they refuse the demon army shelter.

I awoke to the sound of two armies at war and jumped to my feet ready to fight but who? Ger who is by far the largest

SHANE

humanoid I have ever seen was motioning to me over the crowd
to come to him. I could not reach him because of the shear
numbers in my way.

  Windrider reached into the crowd and pulled me out saying need
of lift boss? Rider and me reached the hall of war where the
plans for combating the demons was well underway.

  Pyro turned to me and said Lord Destiny I was about to send a
messenger to request your presents.

  That's not necessary now Pyro I said.

Pyro told me all that had transpired while I slumbered.

  What do you want me to do prince, I asked?

 Nothing. This is not your fight, I have call for this so it is mine to
deal with. I only asked this, if I should loose, do not let the
demons have our families. Although I wanted to help I could feel
my omniscient brother lord Truth about me.

  Truth said, this is what you have worked for, these people have
tasted peace and are willing to die to keep it so.

   Just prior to dawn a the castle was battle ready, as were
every person in it for the forth come battle. I watched as
Pyro dressed in magic armor led his storm troop of loyal men
(the one with him when he was captured by Ger) out the gate
and into the sky by yelling "To wing, to death, to victory".

118

SHANE

There was a great cheer and Pyro was gone into the sky. When the last of the squadrons had left to joint the battle I called Ger and Windrider to the main gate and told them to stand just outside of it.

Rider said, lord we agreed not to join the fight.

Yes, that is true but those filthy God forsaken demons don't know that.

They both smiled at me and Rider said, " your one sweet smart mo'fo Sean.

Ger said, as long as the demons think that the fire army have two titans in reserve they won't come near the castle, very clever indeed master.

I said, well boys there's more to war than just fighting.

Battle and bloodshed went on for three week without intermission. Pyro had been badly hurt twice but still led the battle without pause. I finally told Rider to fetch him for me. When Pyro came before me he was really pissed about my interference. I touched him and his wounds healed.

Then I said, I have not broken my promise but there is something you should know. Truth has informed me that the demons are being magically protected from harm or death while your forces are not. What do you want to do about this Pyro, I said?

119

SHANE

He sat and though a moment and said , there are two ways I could fairly deal with this without your entering the fight. First, I could surrender but that's not going to happen. Second, you could destroy there magic item to make this a fair fight.

Number two it is then I said walking out on to my balcony. I waved my hand and for a brief moment the demons all stood still as if grabbed then the fighting resumed only now the demons were falling to the much more fierce Firewitchs they faced.

The battle end only four hours later and the demons had either fled or been killed by the fire army.

That evening we all sat in a great hall waiting to sup when a lone demon walked right up to me and said, you used your powers to beat our army.

No, foolish demon all I did was remove your spell of protection so it was a fair fight. Besides your army out numbered the princes twenty to one and you still lost.

The demon had not noticed he was standing under the great titan of the air until Windrider said , may I eat him lord?

Perhaps but not yet, I want to ask a few question first. Why are you here?

The demon said, if your going to feed me to that, then why should I answer?

SHANE

If you answer your death will be swift and painless, however if you stall it will be very slow and incredibly painful.

I wanted to see Destiny before I die there is a matter I wish to discuss. Where is he little human, the demon asked as he looked around for some great figure to step forth but none did? I sat there wanting to come up with something to say that was both witty and true to make the demon see the face of the Destiny he now asked for.

I laughed as I stood, friends this one wants to know where he may find Lord Destiny. Oh and I am a puny human? The Firewitchs laughed hard and long. Sky came up followed by her soon to be mate Pyro and they sat with me.

Pyro said , demon did you not say that it was Sean's magic lost the war for you?

I did, said the demon. Well, was your magic so weak that a mere tiny unimposing human could snuff it out? At this the titans that follow me roared their approval of the direction Pyro was going with his questions. The demon jumped to his feet looking as if he had been tagged and said, next to Bnurr the troll no one in this world has a mastery of magic to even rival much less snuff my own.

Very nicely put, a lie, but no less nicely put, You see demon, said Sky, there are many powerful mage and sorcerers on our world and I can feel their presence when they are near, You are not

SHANE

among them lackey for the real wizard.

The demon admitted that although he did have magic skills he was only sent to find out who Destiny was then kill him.

 Ger said, a fools errand demon, Destiny is invulnerable to physical harm and only God has the power to take him another way. However the Christ would not because Sean was chosen to be the lord of Destiny. What shall we do with the assassin loyal friend?

 I say we eat him, said Rider.

That is always your idea because you'll do the eating, said Ger.

Sky suggested that we cleanse his mind and send him back to kill his master.

Justice appeared over our heads and said hello father, Justice would be served if Sky's suggestion is followed.

  We sent the demon back to do what he had been to us to do. Night fell once more and you could find me in the window looking out at the stars.

 Homesick Sean?

 I think that would be safe to say, I said turning to face Pyro.

Your coming here has put me in a place I never thought I would
122

SHANE

be, thank you for everything.

 Kid you didn't need me to help you, your a natural leader and would have been recognized sooner or later.

 Perhaps I would have but you made sure I was.

It was nothing kid forget it, I said.

 He stood there in the shine of the stars looking at me as if I were his father going off to war and never coming home again, then he must have gotten the courage to ask and receive the answer.

 Your going to leave soon aren't you?

 I am on a quest, and have to complete it so I can go home. When are you going to leave?

 Tonight, the longer I wait the harder it will be to go and leave my friend here.

 Pyro had all of the people in the castle lined up to say goodbye when I arrived at the gate. Sky was the first to bid me farewell by kissing me and saying that her life is complete because of me, tossing a lusty look at Pyro, who returned the thought in kind.

 The king shook my hand and said that as long as he lives their will be peace in the Fire Kingdom.

SHANE

Ger stepped forth and knelt because of his great size and said I would go with you if I could but that damn barrier prevents it.

Here take this key and hang it around your neck and you can breech the barrier, I said. Promise me that you will not kill Vapor the gate keeper before I am through with him.

Ger said, on my life I will not until you say Little Lord Destiny, my good friend. He stood again not wanting me to see the tears in his giant red eyes.

Windrider sat on the floor and said knowing you has hurt my diet Sean but it has also made life come full circle and I can enjoy just living and being with Ger in this land. It is all because of you that we are all happy and no longer at war or just plain lonely. Do you want a lift to the portal gateway?

I said yes old friend and here is a portal key for you like the one I gave Ger so you can't be trapped again by anyone. Further, these keys will help you find me if need be, just think about me and I shall appear.

He just looked at me the way Pyro had but he did not take the opening that the silence gave, but stayed silent from the sadness of my departure.

The way back took a few days by air but I did not speak although all of the Firewitchs followed Rider to the portal to bid me a final ado. I waved a final goodbye and stepped though the

124

SHANE

portal but I was not in the land of shadows where I met the
winged titan Windrider. I was standing in the hall of Vapor the
gate keeper.

Vapor, where are you?

He did not answer but I did find a note. It said, follow your heart
and you'll complete the second task. I believed this to be some
sort of trick because my heart is back with Nicky and I can't go
there. I suddenly heard someone crying. Following the sound I
came to a gateway that said, Beware no magic will work beyond
this corridor. I stepped through without a moment to loose, not
thinking about the possible danger I might face.

SHANE

SHANE

CHAPTER 5: The Monster Within.

   The place that I now found myself in was a cross between Shadow land and Sunshine World. It had mountains that kissed the sky and rivers that were the most crystal blue shade you ever could imagine. A familiar sound brought me back to earth from the heights where my soul was instantly lifted. That is when, I remembered the crying. Setting out to investigate the waling, I heard what seemed like crying all around me but it was only the echo's of whoever was doing the actual ballin. I marked where I was incase I had to make a quick get away through the portal. Climbing the mountain I began to wonder if I was still invulnerable, if what I did was considered magic.

   The crying was very near now and I was anxious to see what was doing all of this wailing. I peered over the ledge I was perched on to see a baby lizard the size of a ten year old human child sitting on a rock just ballin it's eyes out.

What's the matter Mony?

   It looked up at me though floods of tears and just froze. It looked more afraid of me than whatever had started the crying in the first place, so I gave communication a second try not knowing if he was even capable of understanding my words.

   Hey, what's the matter lil Mony, I said? It started to move. I jumped down beside him and said don't be afraid Mony.

SHANE

Who's Mony, it said?

I probably looked a little surprised that English came out of his mouth, especially because he was a giant iguana, but I answered him anyway.

Well since I don't know who you are lil guy, Mony will do.

I am to young for a name yet, said the lil lizard boy.

Then Mony it is pal. Now tell your ol' buddy Sean what your troubles are.

Well, some people were trying to capture me for the games.

Tell me what the games are, Mony, I asked?

He said, people take dragons to fight in an arena for money, and if you loose you die unless you fought very well.

No way, what the hell do they do that for, I thought.

Dragons are all slaves here but you would know because your a people.

Well I have an idea lil Mony would you say your mine
so that no one can hurt you. Mony agreed when I told him
that I was going to help him find his family. Further I would
teach him to fight so good that nobody could beat him in a fight.

128

SHANE

He liked the sound of that but didn't like the part about my owning him.

Suit yourself I said as I walked away.

 No wait I think it would be ok, but I'm to little to fight anyone.

Well how big are fighting dragons? Mony said, they are two times you in stature and ten times you in weight I think.

Well, that mean they are about eleven feet tall and fifteen hundred pounds. How long does it take a lil dragon to get that big?

 It will take me six moons, he said.

Six months, I said great now what am I going to do with you until then?

Train me of-course, said Mony.

The next month I did the near impossible, I trained a lil dragon in the Gung-Fu arts of self defense. Further, the little monster learned quickly and grew at a frightening pace without much in the way of food. One very dark night after I made Mony practice his fire breathing skills, I asked will you develop wings?

Maybe, one in every three hundred babies get wings, but nobody knows until the last month of growth was his answer.

SHANE

Then maybe you'll get wings, I said.

No, not me said Mony.

Don't be so damn negative. Why not, I asked him.

 Well, mostly the dragons with wings are born in rich peoples
stables and I'm only a scrappy mountain dragon.

I said, Mony rich people probably buy the winged dragons
because only they can afford to.

 Mony said that seemed reasonable.

One day while we stopped to train Mony on forest fighting we
met a strange man who show more than a small interest in Mony.

 He boldly walked up and grabbed Mony and tried to open his
mouth and look at his teeth. Mony grabbed the man by his neck
and threw him about ten feet behind where Mony was standing.
The man got up and brandished a whip heading for Mony. I cut
him off by walking right up between them.

Just what the hell do you think your going to do with that whip
pal?

 I'm going to teach that blasted dragon some manners.

 Oh, is that right, well of-course you don't think I would kill you
for whipping my dragon?

130

SHANE

I have every right he insulted me.

Oh, is that right, well correct me if I'm wrong but wasn't it you who walked up and start pulling on him?

In fact, your lucky I told him not to kill anyone or you'd be dead instead of insulted.   Let me add this stranger, if you lay one finger on my dragon I'll hit you so damned hard your kids will be born dizzy!!

 The man took a long look at me and said, on the worst day of my life I think I could beat the shit out of you.

OH, is that right, well here let me make a counter proposal.

Today IS the worst day of your life because I'm going to beat the crap out of you! At that I hit him in three places before he even started to get his hands up.

 He pulled a knife and said now your finished.

 He lunged at me but I sidestepped the attempt and tripped him. When he hit the ground I canon balled in the middle of his back. He passed out. When he came to I had take his clothes, money, food, and knife. Because he was tied up he didn't seem to mind.

 Hey Mony, our guest is up.

  There was no need for me to explain what had happened to the

131

SHANE

strange man, he knew he was dead.

 I walked over to him with his knife in my hand and said,
what should I do with you friend after all you were trying to
kill me?

 He said, don't talk me to death just get it over with!

Ok, have it your way pal, I lifted the knife in a striking posture
and cut him free. He rolled over and looked at me in total
surprise.

I said, get up, What's your name?

I am called Lok. Lok hold out your hand. He did so and I cut the
palm of his hand with the knife then I said, I am Sean and cut my
hand. He looked confused until I grabbed his hand in mine and
said, now that our blood has run together we are brothers and
must look out for each other.

 He smiled and said, I get it.

You either had to kill me or make me beholden to you.

Lok, you don't owe me anything and I gave him the knife back.

 Lok proved to be a better cook than Mony or I so he hung
around to make sure us helpless children made it to the city. My
best guess was that I was a curiosity to him.

132

SHANE

Mony however told me if he made one false move he would eat his heart and he said it right to Lok's face.

Lok also found Mony a very strange dragon in that he was not afraid of people at all, in fact quite the contrary.

The three of us travel until we reached a small town. One of the towns people saw Mony and asked me if we would like to challenge.

I said, challenge who?

Lok spoke right up and said, we have a great one here pointing to Mony and you'll have to have something we want to bother with a small match before dragon arena next moon.

The man told Lok thinking he was the owner that they had a dragon who is a retired champion of the dragon war games ten years running.

I said something to Mony and the man told me to be quiet when and the owners were dealing. I walked until my feet were on top of his and said I am the owner pal and if you don't want to be crippled you better apologize.

Lok put his hand on my shoulder and said my brother is telling the truth and he is the greatest human fight who ever walked this land.

The man curtly apologized, then offered both Mony and I a

SHANE

match. I told him that I would think about it if I was fed and watered by a pretty girl. He made it so, we were treated like visiting royalty.

 Lok told me quietly that if we won they will probably try to have us killed before we can tell of their towns defeat.

 Why I asked?

 It is because fighting is our way, the best fighters rule the land as do their dragons, only the dragons don't get the benefits of their fights as humans do.

 We dined at the table of the towns most famous and successful fighter Del. Tar. He was enormous and had no charm to him save that he treated his baby pet dragon very well.

 He looked at Mony and said, this one will die if he fights Yaru the champion. Then he looked at me and said it is best that you don't fight me little puny man I don't wish to kill you.

Thank you Del Tar but you have just convinced me to fight myself and Mony tomorrow, I said with a smile.

 Then tomorrow we fight Stranger, was Tar's answer.

  The sun came up in the sky at half past five bells, very soon for this region I was told.

Lok said as he got up, remember what I said about running for

SHANE

it. Yeah, I do. That was only if Mony won, if you win everything here is your.

What does that mean exactly, I said as I stretched?

Lok said, it means the houses, animals, dragons, and the people.

No kidding Lok, I said as I poked him in the shoulder.

Honest Indian, Sean. However, if you loose and Mony wins Del Tar gets Mony and me, he said sternly so that I would remember what was at risk here.

Gee, thanks for the pep talk Lok, I said as I grimaced.

In the late morning we went to the arena where we would fight for our lives this day. Mony was so scared that he started peeing ever few minutes.

I went over to him and said, your almost at you full growth and who could possibly be better trained than you? Yaru is going to run right at you because that is how all dragons are taught to fight. I want you to side step and trip him. Once he is on the ground twist his arm and lock it the way I taught you and you win without killing.

Mony said, what if he gets a hold of me and pushes me down?

Spin the way I taught you and he will flip off of you, then use

SHANE

your kicking and punching skills to whip his butt, I coached!

The caller who would announce the fighters and whatever rules
were agreed upon, called Yaru and Mony to the center of the
arena for there instructions.

 I told Mony to go Far and kick ass, at which he gave me claw
 (the equivalent of a human five).

Del Tar arranged for Lok and me to sit next to him in the seats of
honor to view the contest. Yaru, who was full grown stood a
head above Mony.

 The bell that marked the beginning of the match sounded and
the two competitors moved forth to engage. Yaru did exactly
what I told Mony he was going to do, he rushed straight forward
in the charge of an angry bull. Mony sidestepped him and
delivered a thrust kick to the kidneys of Yaru who went down.
Yaru got up smiling because he had been wrong in thinking that
the smaller Mony would be an easy mark in the wins column.
Yaru ran at Mony again but with care this time trying to grab
on so he could use his greater size. Mony allowed Yaru to come
within finger distance then delivered a devastating sidekick
which lifted Yaru up and threw him on his back. Mony ran over
to where Yaru landed waiting for him to trying to get up. Yaru
not realizing that Mony was just behind him attempted to get
up. Mony spun and swept Yaru out then jumped on his chest
pinning his arms, Mony began to beat Yaru about the head and
shoulders violently. Yaru was beaten.

SHANE

Del Tar stood and said kill Yaru if he isn't dead!

No, he is mine by right of victory to do with as I will, I heatedly interjected.

Right you are, I apologize said Tar.

Mony, helped the bigger dragon up and took Yaru to the creek on the edge of town and cleaned him up. Lok, went to supervise, or at least that is what everyone thought. Lok looked confused at me as I gestured to get out of here to him, then suddenly understood that I was providing them with a means of escape if I lost my fight.

Del Tar did not catch on to my plan and Lok, Mony, and Yaru escaped.

Del Tar said to me are you ready to die.

I just smiled and showed the usual martial arts salute that I did just before I engage in a fight. Del looked at me as if I had three heads when I did it, but it didn't seem to change his posture at all. The arena looked bigger from the stands than it did from the ground where I now stood.

The announcer said something but I could only think will I ever see my little Nicky again.

Hey, said Del Tar, let's go the fight has been started boy.

SHANE

I thought to myself he could have just rushed me but instead he
warns me to be on guard, I won't kill this man for that kindness.

Del Tar was one very big man and had reportedly had two
hundred forty six previous bouts killing all but two men in a fair
fight. I walked up to where he stood in the center of the arena.
I indicated that I was ready to have a go as did he.

Del Tar lunged with a demon speed that I would not have
thought possible of a man of his size. I just stepped sideways
and tripped him. He regained his feet instantly and tried to kick
me but I blocked his kick with one of my own then delivered a
second kick to his nose, which broke it. I did not wait for him to
recover, I kicked him in his knee braking it.

Del Tar was hurt very bad but still he fought on with vigor. I
kicked him in the face five times fast then one more time as
hard as I could. Del Tar went down and did not move, so I went
over to see if he was dead. When I bent over him, he grabbed
me and started to squeeze hard to brake my ribs but I delivered
a head butt to his already busted nose and he let go.

I pulled Del Tar up to his knees and began to beat him with my
hands until his eyes rolled up and he fell. This time he was not
faking and the town official declared me the winner.

Del Tar came to in his bed with a great grown and said I must
have won, I still live.

No, you lost big guy but I don't kill unless I have no other

SHANE

choice.

Tar looked at me and said I and all I have are yours master.

I know Tar but I am going to leave and you must rule in my place with justice and mercy until I come back.

What if you do not, asked Tar?

That is why you will rule in my stead but with mercy not violence. Do you swear it will be so Del Tar?

Yes, Del Tar gives you his Word.

Lok my brother will be back if I do not and he is to be treated as you would treat me, as the lord of this place second only to me. Do you also swear to protect and serve Lok?

Yes, I so swear, said Tar.

Good you rest and heal I must go now, I said, then I turned and went to find my little band of friend who were laying in the weeds, if you know what I mean..

I found Lok and the two dragons on the trail that led out of town towards the next.

Lok said, did you loose Sean?

No, I won, I said.

SHANE

Then why are we leaving, asked Mony?

Because we didn't come here to stay remember. Further, I now
own all of that town and Del Tar who has sworn his allegiance to
you and me second lord of the dragons.

 What, I am also lord there in that town, asked Lok in
jest?

 Yes, your my brother remember, I can't allow anyone to show
you disrespect because it makes me look bad, I explained.

    Later that day when we stopped to have our dinner Lok asked
me to, teach me to fight like me. I told him that I would on
one condition that he only teaches it to people of good hearts or
dragons of the same. He gave you me his word.

 Yaru, how do you feel, I inquired?

 He said, Old, young master I got wiped by a dragon half my size
when I use to be a champion.

 Yaru you got beat by my training as did Del Tar. There is no
shame in it for you, still you have knowledge that I need of the
towns, world and there games, I told him. Further, I need
someone for my other dragon to practice with and in that you
will learn to fight my way which will make you great again.

 The journey took us to a town that had heard the way me and

SHANE

my dragon had swept cleanly through Del Tar's best and they were afraid so they were looking for giants. WE walked right in to the town square where Lok jumped up on a rock.

"Behold the best fighters in the land are here".

 A old man said where are they, I see only a foundling dragon and a little man.

 Yaru said, old fool I am Yaru the destroyer, champion of a hundred dragon fights and at my best I could not beat Mony the small.

Moreover, said Lok, no five of you could beat Master Sean!

 The towns people knew of Yaru and were excited to see him but gave us no regard at all which pissed off Lok.

 I said, be calm and find this towns greatest fighter and insult him into a fight with me. Also get a bout for Mony will ya, I think I am going to find lodgings for us.

 I was given a large house at the edge of town to use in honor of Yaru. For the first time in what seemed like a life time I laid down in peace to sleep. My dreams were all of my family and what had previously transpired. Lok asked around the town for the best fighters, finding them easily because they were all very cocky and arrogant. Lok promptly told them that they all fight like wenches. They rushed him in the heat of their anger and pinned him to a table.

SHANE

Hey, boys what'cha doing with that dude on the table, asked Mony?

Piss off they said without turning around.

Mony walked up and picked two of them by their heads saying, I asked you a question politely and you diss me. Hey, I don't think so! Now gentleman let my master's brother go or I'll flash fry you all with my fiery breath.

They let Lok go who punched one guy in the stomach so hard he coughed up blood. Lok is a big man after all.

Lok said, if any of you tough guys want to fight, me and my brother will take you all on for everything you own. Oh yeah, my dragon friend can whip any dragon you got. With that said they drifted.

Deep in a calm restful slumber Lok told our companions to leave me to rest for once because I never got any quality sleep.

Ripped from my rest in the early morn, I sprang from my bed and rushed out the door to see a mob outside my door in a fever for blood.

What do you want, I said as I yawned? One man raised his hand and all fell silent. We are here to answer the challenge thrown down by your foolish brother, he said with conviction!

142

SHANE

What is that exactly, Asked?

He said that he and you could beat all of us, we except your challenge. I just shook my head and shrugged my shoulders, then I closed the door and went back to bed, because I was too damn tired to worry about it now.

The challenge was set for the following morning.

I went and woke up Lok and ask him if he lost his bloody mind to challenge all the fighting men in town at once.

Mony rolled over in his blanket on the floor and told me what happened to Lok.

I guess I don't blame you bro, but we are in a bad way here, there are so many of them and so few of me and you. We better go over strategy, everybody up, I shouted!

All day we practiced our back to back fight skills and the way we would keep them at bay while picking them off. Lok was learning so fast that I had taught him several advanced Kajukenbo tricks, which he seemed to be able to use proficiently.

Very good Lok, your getting this at a fevers pace which is good because we don't have much time, I said with a little, very little relief.

That night Yaru watched over us while we slept so that no one could harm us. Someone tried at about four in the morn but Yaru

SHANE

burned up his head when it came through my window.

 I sat up and Yaru smiled and said, sleep master no one will get in the house this night.

Morning zoomed in on us before it usual did and we got up. The fight was not until noon so I prepared myself for death. I asked my friends to leave me until a half hour before the fight in solitude. I dressed in my fighting togs then I knelt and prayed to God that we would not parish in this endeavor but would also not be forced to kill needlessly. The remainder of the morning I stretched and meditated. The time came for me to Go, so Mony knocked on my door. They all looked surprised when I appeared in the door way wearing fighting togs that they had never seen and I had matching sets for each of them. The dragons wore vests and capes and Lok and I wore silk Kajukenbo fighting gear. I taped Lok's hands while I explained that this is necessary because we are fighting against impossible odds.

Then he taped my hands and ankles as explain how to do it for maximum effect. The hour of the fight came near and the towns people were piling into the local arena. A man from the town fighting council came to fetch Lok and I. Mony almost killed him for approaching without being announced. The man quickly explained who he was and asked if we were ready to compete.

 Yaru said we will be there shortly, now leave us.

We entered through the side door so that nobody would notice

SHANE

our presence. They announced everyone of our opponents names and there were many. Finally the announcer said our names and we entered. I told Lok to stay close to me, then I walked right into the middle of all of our foes and Lok took my back. The horn sounded and Lok kicked a guy in the face, who fell without moving upon the ground.

Meanwhile, I sent three bold fools to see the sandman. Further, upon the four men hitting the ground all the other combatants jumped back out of reach. We were not having much trouble with them because they were not use to fighting as a unit and we were.

Fifteen minutes into the match we were doing well but we were getting tired because overwhelming number of guys who stood against us. Lok yelled start killing them or they are going to kill us.

 I said, I don't want to kill anyone without just cause. I held up my arms and said if you let my brother go I will let you execute me.

 Lok sprang forth to my side pushing the person closest to me down. Are you crazy, you can't let yourself get butchered just to save us, after all I got you into this.

 A large man in the center of our foes yelled stop and everybody did.

 You would die to save this braggart when you are obviously the

SHANE

best fighter on the field today?

 Yes, He is my brother so his life is more important to me than my own.

  The large man said, let it be done than and the contest was over.

  The room I was led to was a very well built prison room with a good bed which I crashed on.

Wake me when it is time for me to go, I said to the guard.

  A voice in my sleep said wake up master we're getting you out of there.

I opened my eyes and said I made a deal. Here I am, here I stay until they kill me.

The voice said I shall miss you master, and I will bow to no other the way I did for you.

  Late evening was across the land when the cell door creaked open hitting the wall with a thud.

Time to go sir, said the guard.

His head was bowed as I walked past him. Another guard grabbed my wrists to bind them and the first guard, said that is not necessary he is here of his own choosing, besides he could

146

SHANE

kill us both if he wanted.

  The second guard acknowledge the fact and he also bowed then.

Well gentlemen let's get on with it, people are expecting to see a killin, so we must not let them down.

The guard turned and said follow me please.

The man who was behind me was the first guard and he said it is a damned shame that your life will end on such a bad note when no man I have ever seen could beat you.

 I said, yeah maybe but where I come from there are a lot of men that could ring me out like a rag.

  You must come from a wondrous place sir.

Yes I do, I said with a smile.

 The lights in the arena were very bright for being torches on the walls. Every person in the town seemed to want to see me die, because they were all in attendance. The big man who I dealt with before was seated just in front of me in the box for the town nobles. He stood up, raised a hand and a silence chocked out the prattle of the multitudes.

You would more than likely beaten all of us if the fight had continued, he said plainly.

147

SHANE

Well I guess that it's a little to late for that,   You honor me
sir, I might have survived but my brother may not have, so I
decided to bargain for his life, I said frankly.

  You are very brave to die for your brother in this matter, he said.

Thank you, but it was your charity that allowed Lok to go free, I
returned.

  Then, he said, how shall you die friend?

  Is old age out of the question, I said?

The stadium was filled with laughter, to a passer by it would
have seemed a celebration not a man's death that was going on
inside.

  When the crowd settled down the big man said, you are equally
as skilled with your whit as your are with a fist. However, a deal
has been made and though it pains me more than I can say
friend, you must be put to death.

  I ask you again to choose the method because I cannot, will not
he said with conviction.

  I looked him in the eye and said, beheading is my chose because
it is swift and painless.

  He said so be it.

148

SHANE

They must have anticipated my method of chose because a large block of wood was brought in and a burly man with a broad axe.

I walked over to the burly man and said may I see your axe? He looked at the man in charge who nodded his approval. I picked it up and inspected the blade sharpness. It was quite sharp and nick free, so I gave it back to the headsman.

The guard escorted me over to the block where I would loose my head. A guard stepped forward and grabbed my hands to tie them. I hit him in the chest knocking him down.

Don't insult me, I have no fear of this axe and I refuse to be bound like an animal. I will place me head on the block and he will strike I said pointing to the headsman.

The burly man held out his hand then said, let me shake the hand of a truly brave man.

I shook his hand then I knelt and placed my head on the block for cleaving. In one swift mighty blow the headsman struck. To the amazement of everyone my head was right were I left it. Further, the axe was deep in the block below my neck, which gave me quite a surprise, so I stood up which scared everyone nearly to the grave. The headsman jumped back and started to pray. Everybody else stayed put except for the big man I had dealt with. He grabbed a bow and arrow which he lit in a brazier next to him and shot me with it. However, the arrow did not find

SHANE

it's mark but fell to dust in front of me.

The man yelled he is **A DEMON FROM HELL** run for your lives!

I wave a hand and all the gates closed. Well how about that my powers have returned. Just at that moment the face of truth appeared over the stadium.

Hello, Destiny long has it been since last we spoke, said a familiar voice.

Truly, it has been to long, why do you come to me now Truth, I asked?

I have come because your task here is finished, as you can see you once more have the full use of your abilities. The truth of it is that this was a barbarous warlike place where might made right. However, you have brought loyalty, mercy, love, compassion and self sacrifice to this land. The seed you have planted will grow forever here in glory with GOD's blessing. You must continue on your task, it is always present in you mind is it not, Truth told me?

Yes, but I feel that the task here needs a little more foundation before I leave, was my answer.

Very well brother I will see you soon, said Truth. With that said he was gone.

Sunshine poured through my bedroom window as the sun pull

150

SHANE

itself over the horizon. I sleep in fanciful dreams of home and Nicky in my arms again. However, there was always something in the back of my mind that said someone is probing you so be aware and defend yourself. Nevertheless, the dream of Nicky was worth a little probing safe or otherwise. I woke to the sound of giggling children at my window. Their small faces smiling over the windowsill at me as I lay sleeping.

I said, do you kids want to see some magik tricks or do you just want to watch me sleep? We want to see the magik Mr. demon sir, said one very small tot.

Ok, magik it is then, I said. I stood on the bed and my clothes dressed me by themselves.

Alright kids what now?

Come outside and play with us.

We all went down where the children swam at, and did most of their playing.

However, the pond was stale and the grass stank, so I decided to change that. I raised my hand and pointed at the river across the field from the pond, lightning sprang from my fingers and cut a dike from the river to the kids pond. I then made a cloud come down and hoist all the children up out of the area that I was remodeling, they loved it. I made the bottom of the pond and dike turn to granite so it would be smooth for the kids. Which was easy because the soil wash gravel rich , I simply fused it.

151

SHANE

There was a big rock by the pond so I remodeled it into a slide for the pond which was more pool than pond now. The towns people who were still very afraid of me came to see what the great noise was.

The burly man noticed that the children were floating on a cloud, fell to his knees and begged me "please don't carry off our children".

I looked at him and laughed, you silly man I am fixing the waterway for the kids to play in. Can you not see the slide I have made for them on? Beside the work I have done on your pond will benefit the whole town.

   The children gathered around me as I told them about my Titans and how I met them.

 After a little while one little boy said, I don't believe there are anything like Titans were you came from.

 His mother grabbed him and beat him because she thought that if I got mad I would destroy them all.

Stop, beating that child woman, I bellowed in a voice that shook the ground.

The woman shook in fear as did all the adult villagers, but the children said thanks for saving him wizard. I smiled at the little boy, who smiled back.

SHANE

Why, I asked? I have come because your task here is to believe.
So, I will help you learn how to.

I waved my hand, for all to see but not understand.

 The air suddenly burst to fire as if the sun had fallen to the
earth. Yet, nobody stirred from the place where they were. A
voice came from the fire and said you have called and I have
come to that summons.... MASTER! Then all was silent.

 Show yourself Titan, I said.

 The people all shook in fear as Windrider materialized in front of
them.

 Master it is good to see you after so long apart, said the mighty
winged Titan.

 I have brought you here for two important reasons. First, is
because I am finished here and wish to leave.

 Rider said, it is done Sean.

 Second, and more important is that a little boy wished to see
a mighty Titan, So I brought you here to show him that anything
is possible if you believe.

 Boy, come here said Windrider to the lil'kid who was looking at
him so intently.

SHANE

It was you who asked for me was it not?

Yes, blurted the boy.

Then come here, Rider said.

The boy walked toward Rider when a person in the crowd said don't it will eat you boy.

Windrider stood up and opened his wings all the way, then he said, if I was hungry I would not choose little meatless children I would want a fat fool like you.

At that he leaned down and looked hard at the person who spoke out.

The man said, it was not I who spoke.

SILENCE WORM, I am a Titan and have ears that can hear an ant fart, so DO NOT LIE TO ME!

The boy flew around the country on Rider's neck for a hour or so then came back to earth. When he got off Windrider, he came to me and said, if you leave will the Titan go to?

Yes, he is my companion and will carry me where I have to venture to finish the quest I am on. However, I have someone that will be your friend above all others if you wish. In fact, he will protect you and make you rich.

154

SHANE

Mony, come here buddy. The dragon came to me and knelt.

 What is your bidding master?

 I didn't get an answer out because the boy cut me off by saying, he can't fly like the Titan, he's just a normal dragon.

 Mony turned to the boy and said, I am no Titan that is true but a truer friend and protector you could not find in this world. Will you except me as your blood brother and companion for life.

The kid looked at me.

 I said, Mony has offered his life to you of his own free will, can you make the same offer to him?

 A long silence fell over the town until the boy said, I am Kel and I will be your blood brother if you wish.

 It is my wish lil' Kel, yet I wish I could offer you wings to carry you to the sky.

Rider said, your going to give a gift to those two are you not.

 Your reading my mind old friend, I said.

 No, I just know your way, said the great man-bat.

 Kel gather all of your people in the arena in one hour, then you and Mony go to the center and wait.

SHANE

The arena seemed strangely hot for some reason that afternoon when all of the terrified people entered. When Kel and Mony were in the middle I spoke.

To these brave souls I will give a gift, to the dragon the best wings there are and to the boy magik to protect this world. I raised my hand and made it so.

SHANE

SHANE

CHAPTER SIX: TITANS

A week after I had given Kel and his winged dragon incredible powers to protect the land they lived in I mounted the giant blood red scourge know as Windrider and departed. I was not needed here and Kel was schooled in the proper use of his might, so I ventured once more on the quest that brought me to this place.

The trip back to the gate that bordered each world was a quiet one that made my winged friend uneasy.

Deep thoughts master?

Yes, I am thinking of home and my mate, who it seems I have been absent from for a thousand year Rider.

Well master, it hasn't been a thousand years, but it has been three since I have met you.

THREE, my God has it been so long Titan?
I am sorry to say that it is, said Rider.

Upon reaching the gate I felt that we would not be alone if we passed through the portal barrier.

I told this to Windrider who roar as a lion would threw his massive teeth, " Finally I'll get some exercise".

158

SHANE

WE entered the gate keeper Vapor's temple to find Ger sitting in the seat where first I saw Vapor.

Brother, roared Rider, it's been to long since we were together!

Boys, hold for a moment we are not alone here, I said.

Ger jumped to his feet and flexed all four of his redwood sized arms, yelling come forth coward or die painfully.

I sincerely doubt that either of you two lummoxes could due me harm, said the voice of our unseen visitor. I made a motion at the Titans that whoever it was could not sense me and to keep up the banter until I found them.

In a dark corner was the visitor that I sought and it did not know I was there until it was way to late to defend itself.
With a wave of my hand the corner was no longer dark and the creature looked me in the face with horror in it's eyes.

Destiny, I did not know you were here, he did not tell this one of your presence here.

Who didn't tell you beast said Ger?

The answer is not yours for the taking Ger of the puny forest Titans, nor for the foul mat-bat who lends not his loyalty to any save himself.

159

SHANE

SILENCE, roared Rider! Master or no, if you utter of that old happen I shall destroy you parasite.

Electricity filled the air, if I wasn't invulnerable it would have Kentucky fried my human shell. The creature in the corner not realizing that both of these Titans were special and had full control of their titan powers which is not generally so, was being very bold. Ger grabbed it and made it a prison of Amber up to it's neck, then tossed it to Rider who was so pissed off he did not hear me ask him to stay his hand momentarily. I had to nailed him in the back with a cold blast, because he was a fire Titan and would respond to the cold unfavorably just to get his attention.

Rider turned to me and said, am I not loyal, do I not do your bidding let me have him!

I said, all you say is true and I feel that somehow he has earned what your going to give him. Yet, I must know why he is here, who he is and who sent him to bushwhack my allies.

Ger said, Rider be calm for awhile then you may have him okay brother.

In a fit of great fear the shadow creature sang like a bird to save his life but Rider would not permit that to happen and in a moment of the most savage brutality ever displayed I had ever witnessed Windrider butchered the creature. However he did not rejoice in his kill as I had expected.

160

SHANE

Ger said, Rider killed not for anger, nor sport or bloodlust but for the honor of his clan.

Tell me of this hap of old that Rider spoke of, I said to Ger.

The tale that was spun made my hair stand up on the back of my neck. The mammoth forest Titan told me of a time long ago when all the land of the Titans were at war and Titans had to choose sides, there was no neutral.

How does that have anything to do with Rider?

Ger sat and said, the Windrider and I have been comrades for as long as my memory is. When the fighting broke out his clan fought for the lords of fire, mine for the Titans of nature. Further, whatever side your are swore to is who you obey. One day during a great battle we met face to face and could not find it in our hearts to trying kill each other. Well, Riders people ordered him to kill me, where my leader told me to follow my heart. More, when Rider refuse to kill his life long friend his clan was disgraced. Nothing more was said.

The information I received from the shadow creature was that Vapor was stirring up trouble in the land of Titans to restart the war they had centuries before.

We must stop Vapor at any cost Lord DESTINY, said Windrider.

Ger agreed that if the Titans went to war this time then Vapor would gain the upper hand on us in some unknown way.

161

SHANE

Suddenly Vapors face appeared and said, well lil' lord Destiny and his lackeys what a surprise. I am of course nowhere near you for safety reasons, yet you have completed two of the three tasks. Now I charge you with this last task fledgling whelp, beat me and maintain the peace among the Titans and I will give you the information you require to find the master key.

He disappeared with a warning, you are not the only near omnipotent being in that land......

Three brave friend enter the portal barrier to the home of the Titans to do battle one last time together in all probability. I asked Ger as we walked if he was the biggest of all the Titans?

Windrider said, no the man-mammoth is the biggest and Ger's swore blood enemy.

Why I asked wryly?

Ger said, long ago he and his clan trampled my elder predecessor.

You mean they killed yer granpappy don't ch'a.

That is correct although Until now I have never heard it put that way before master, Ger said.

The days were long and hot. The countryside was beautiful and smelled of flowers of all sorts. However, food was not something

SHANE

we had in surplus.

I'm so damn hungry I could eat the bark off of those trees over there boys, I don't know about you but I simply starving!

Rider replied, yes I too need meat to sate my ravenous appetite, what of you Ger.

I get most of my food from light like a plant or in my case a tree, said Ger, so I need little in the way of actual food brother.

It nigh midday when we reached the home of Ger's people.

They looked very carefully at me, paying little in the way of attention to Rider since he was Ger's best bud.

What is that asked one of the clan? Before Ger could answer it grabbed for me. I hit it with a blast of concentrated air knocking it on it big ass.

Keep your hands to yourself Chester, I said.

The Titan jumped to his feet and started to give me the bums rush when Ger clothes lined the bastard, buttering the ground with him.

The big Titan said why did you interfere Ger?

TO SAVE YER STINKING LIFE FOOL, he growled through boulder sized teeth.

163

SHANE

What could one puny lil' piss-ant of a human do to me Unsavory of fools?

Rider said, he is lord Destiny friend and could wipe his bum with your head if he so wishes.

All of the Titans look hard at me to see if Rider could possibly be telling the truth.

Night Blew across the land like a hurricane, all was dark in minutes from the onset of dust.

That was fast, I said.

You are not in Kansas anymore so stop thinking like a human master, said Ger.

Tell me Ger how did you come to be in the land of Bnurr the troll.

That was Vapor's doing, he desecrated a temple here and I was sent after him to bring him back for justice, I failed.

Then Windrider came looking for me and he to got trapped by that son of a bitch Vapor. Anyway we leave tomorrow for the great hall where the council of regents will want to hear of your quest and the deeds of Vapor.

The trio set out at dawn for a point some ten days journey

SHANE

for a Titan, so I rode on Riders back. It was midmorning when
we met the man-mammoth in the road.

   So, you have come back coward to face me at last.

   Ger turned to Rider and said, get Sean the hell out of here it's
a trap!

   Rider grabbed me and shot skyward yelling I'll be right there to
help you.

   No, stay away I want him to myself.

   Rider can Ger take this sucker, I mean he's pretty damn big and
looks as mean as a rattler.

Yeah, he'll take'm because he hates him so much that he has no
concern for his own life which will give him an big ass
advantage.

   The two mastodons circle each other for a few moments in an
effort to size up the others attack plan, then suddenly with
a fury I had not thought possible they began. With each blow
came the sound of hard rolling thunder, another and another.
Just then I saw two Titans hiding in the trees behind Ger who
was as far as I could tell winning. One thrust out a huge arm and
stabbed Ger in the back.

   No, I yelled, Then I stood on the back of Rider raised my hands
to heaven and brought forth an onslaught of un-dream able

165

SHANE

savage power.

 You would take from me a dear friend in the name of murder, I
SAY NO!!!!!!

 Lightning slammed into the earth and shook the ground, The soil
was rent apart like an earthquake.

 The surrounded devastation was more than a mile wide in any
direction and at least a mile deep into the ground. The two
bushwhackers were sent express mail to the promised land. The
mammoth stood shaking in fear from the seen he just witnessed,
and even my Titan friend seemed a little leery of me at the
moment.

 Ger are you okay buddy?

 Yes, apparently your giving me the key to move from one plain
to the next has the side effect of invincibility, I am not harmed at
all master.

 The great man-bat landed near Ger, then sat looking at the
cowering mammoth before us.

 I wouldn't have believe anyone or thing could make ol'hosenose
grovel like this, said Rider.

Truly I should say The man-mammoth was the biggest creature I
have ever seen. He was at the least 10 feet taller than Ger and
twice his weight. He had the head of a wooly mammoth and

166

SHANE

shoulders, But the body a super giant man. He was proud and exuded power and strength.

It is not for you I grovel worm but before the endless might of Destiny, said mammoth.

How do you know that I am Destiny I asked the huge Titan?

Only a key master would be able to control such terrifying powers.

Who sent you here to greet us mammoth?

Vapor did, he has a magik item that makes him more powerful than anyone I thought I would ever see. I was wrong none could stand before such power as you have.

Maybe, maybe not we shall see.

Ger what should we do with him, after all he is your enemy?

Let him go, I don't need his blood on my hands to know that I had him beat before I got stabbed, said Ger.

The man-mammoth looked at Ger and said, I did not mean to trample your grand-sire, I am poor of sight and can not stop easily once I am at a full run. I was suddenly just there and I could not stop. In my youthful pride I thought since I had such a great size and strength I could get away from admitting my wrongfulness. I am sorry for your loss.

167

SHANE

He simple turned and stamped out of the valley.

Two hours went by before Rider got up enough courage to ask his question.

Master, how great is the burden your carrying as the Key of Destiny, he said.

Friend, I don't think I could express the sheer might that I feel within me or the fine line of controlling that might, the burden is great, I only let loose for an instant back there and look at the carnage it cause. No, no I dare not ever let completely loose or all you see would be gone.

Ger broke in by saying, it's a damn good thing your on our side Sean or our nuts would be in the gravy.

We all laughed like we did so long ago without care, only joy was in our minds, a great feeling if only for a moment.

The sun had came and set four times since we had last seen hide nor hair of life, yet we were being watched by strong eyes constantly and it made all of us edgy. That dark night whatever it was decided now was the time to come in to do it's job.

It crept in and sprinkled some dust over each of our sleeping forms then said what good is your magik if you can't wake.

A good point, said Ger, but we aren't asleep assassin.

168

SHANE

The small winged bear turned to fly away and came face up on Rider who smiled and said, think again.

I stepped out of the dark into the fire near the Titans and said, I always put a protect shield around us when we sleep so your plan would not work even if we were sleeping.

The bear said, I didn't have much chose, it was do or die, I chose do so Vapor wouldn't kill me.

Can't blame him ya know, he doesn't have the means to protect himself from that jerk Vapor, said Rider. Just let him go

PLEASE, I WILL SPRED THE WORD OF YOU KINDNESS!

Would the hurt our cause or strengthen it I asked my titan friends.

Strengthen, said Ger in his usual baritone.

So we let the bear creature go.

The last day of travel to the great hall came and went uneventfully. When we approached the gate to the entrance of the hall itself we were greeted by big angry gorilla type guards who bowed as Ger walked forth and again as Windrider passed, yet they jumped in my way and said stop mortal you may not pass.

SHANE

I smiled curtly then blasted them out of my way.

See ya, I said as I passed by their shaking bodies.

Outside the hall looked old and rundown, but inside it was rich and lavish, It would have made any king jealous. Once totally inside the hall I treated quite nicely, like visiting royalty.

A very old Titan said, welcome lord Destiny we are honored by your presence.

Glad to be here, heard your having trouble with a titan named VAPOR!!!!

The hall was so silent that you could hear a mouse fart when Vapor himself answered me.

Yes, that is so lil' Destiny said Vapor.

I raised my hand to cast and Ger placed his hand over mine and shook his head no.

Have you lost your mind Ger, he is our enemy, I said.

Ger said,. no fighting can be done in here master.

He released my arm and I said I apologize I was unaware of your customs and I sat.

Vapor took center stage and started spouting hatred at all of

SHANE

the delegates that were not loyal to him(it was obvious he meant for war to be the result of his insults). Not one delegate seemed to be moved by his browbeating. I however could see into his mind and knew these weren't just words but a declaration of war against all of creation that didn't follow him. I got a belly full of his venom, so I got up to stretch my legs for awhile.

After leaving the hall I found a quiet place and said, TRUTH I need your wisdom.

Truth's face appeared in front of me and said no he doesn't have the master key you seek brother, but your still going to have to deal with him because he know who does have it. At this moment he is using the magik charm he was given by your true foe, so help the Titans and be well and he was gone.

The hall was amiss when I returned, Vapor was using an amulet to cloud the judgment of the delegates.

I believe that you will find that Vapor is using magik on you, I said.

With a wave of my hand his amulet was destroyed and the delegates were pissed because Vapor dare use his powers in the great hall. Vapor and all his minions hauled out of there in a fever pitch. Meanwhile, in the hall I was making sure everything was okay.

The oldest Titan came over to me and said you too used your

powers here but for our good so we find no fault in your actions.

Will there be war now, I asked.

More than likely, he said.

War came in the days that followed, Vapor was extremely adept at waging war and devising tactics for his massive horde of followers. Although, Vapor's forces out numbered Ger's armies and Rider's Airforce the war was evenly matched for some reason.

Battles went on night and day for two years before there was decisive victory. Vapor had captured Ger's family and put them to death, this drove him wild. Rider and Ger let loose all the might of the horrid powers I helped to unlock within themselves. They razed the strongholds of their enemy and all the land between them. None who stood against them were given quarter.

Forty day passed and the troops of Vapor were dead or captured, but not Vapor himself.

Vapor finally came forth and said, I challenge Ger to a winner take all fight to the death.

Ger except of coarse, and the battle was on. To my utter amazement Ger was Getting rang out like a dirty rag, he was even bleeding which is impossible.

SHANE

Suddenly JUSTICE sprang forth and said father Vapor is using a magik item to kill Ger, you must take him this madness has gone long enough.

Truth also appeared and added the truth is that Vapor is true evil and must be stopped if we are to set the balance back right.

As I walked down on to the battle field Truth and Justice lit up the entire sky as if the sun had just come up.

Vapor, you are judged to have no good in you, so I who am Destiny the living Fate for all charge you to defend yourself villain. Ger was scooped up off the ground by Rider and flown clear of harms way.

Vapor said you cannot harm me peon I am all powerful.

No, your not, only God is all powerful and he is not with you Vapor.

He raised his hands and began to cast. A million shards of metal hurled toward me. I waved my hand and the shards fell to dust. Then I cast a beam of ice at Vapor. He broke it by calling down lightning. He smiled then he cast a cloud of poison at me. I shook my head at how dumb he was, I waved my hand and the wind blew the cloud back over Vapor.

Okay, enough farting around prepare to meet your maker boy. All the air was alive with energy, Vapor threw all the power at his

SHANE

command. I just stood there and let it hit me .

When the watchers of the battle could see clearly they saw Vapor standing on the field bragging that he had kill Destiny. However, when he pointed to where I used to be and I was still there to his utter horror.

YOU HAVE DONE ALL THAT YOU COULD BUT NONE MAY ESCAPE DESTINY.....PREPARE TO DIE.

Vapor screamed in horror as my eyes turn red and start crackling with energy. The ground began to quake and thunder began to roll clouds moved in and I was the sky for the moment, Vapor looked up at me. I had to his horror absorbed his blast and now was going to deliver it to him. I closed my eyes, then opened my arms and eyes at the same time blasting everything in front of me for a thousand miles to sand. Vapor was gone, and I closed my arms, IT IS DONE, I said in a thunderous voice.

Justice landed by me and said you know that there was no choice.

Will I ever finish shit so I can go home, son?

Destiny you know as well as I that there is no going back, said Truth.

I sat down and cried for my lost loves, Nicky I will find a way back to you I swear it. The land behind me where Vapor had been was not unlike Japan after they dropped the bomb, only it

174

SHANE

was a thousand times as bad. Ger and the others stood looking
at the deed and thought to themselves so this is what letting
loose looks like. There was no life, just a dust like sand for miles
in every direction, Death and nothing more.

   No, it is not, said Truth, he still did not loose control of the
tirade within him.

 Scary to think that only one man could do this with a single
thought isn't it, Justice said as a solitary tear ran down his face.

 Upon finishing the task of securing peace for the Titans
my work here was done and I still didn't know what or where
I was going. Yet, I know I must go on to set the balance right
again. The road always beckons to me, so I go...

SHANE

SHANE

CHAPTER SEVEN: SOLITUDE

   For the first time I felt truly alone, with the titans
staying in their land and my brothers off on their own tasks.
I sit here in the portal of time and space thinking over the
last words said to me by TRUTH," the answer will come from
within you, ponder this brother".

   In this hall there are so many portal ways that it would take a
million lifetimes to search them all, and I didn't know if I had that
much time. As I walked down the long corridors of doors I could
not tell which of these portals I should take. Finally, I began to
feel a strong pull toward a corner of the great hall that I hadn't
explored yet.   So strong was the feeling that I stumbled and fell
against the wall like drunk fresh from the bar.

   The words of Truth came hauntingly poring back to me," From
Within ". I followed the impulse carefully down the passageway,
incase it was a trap and assassins were waiting. Upon nearing
my goal the sensation multiplied. Before me was a small beam
of light beckoning me forth. My sense of danger warned me not
to break the beam, however, the sensation in my stomach(a gut
feeling if you will) commanded me on.   I knelt to inspect the
origin of the beam, I could see none. Raising a hand I broke
the tiny beam of light. At once I had regretted it.

Endless seas of sand as far as the eye could span surrounded

SHANE

me in every direction. The hall that I had stood in moments
before was nowhere to be seen. A moments reflection on
listening to one's sense of danger seem prudent.

  Sol beat down with a vengeance that day. I was nearly burn
to a crisp in less than an hour. There was no visible shade or
structure anywhere, so I determined that if I was going to
see anymore tomorrows I better hit the brick. Hours passed and
still no life or structures were evident. Fatigue set in as did
dehydration. I walked until I could not stand then I crawled, not
wanting to give in to my fate.

  Finally, I was finished, one step away from heat stroke and one
foot in the grave. Laying there looking at the sunny sky I felt the
way a new born babe feels, alone and confused. Resigned to my
predicament, I closed my eyes and thought of home and Nicky.

  At one point I thought I heard Truth say to Justice we can't
interfere in this matter, then oblivion....

  Shivering, my eyes painfully opened and surveyed the area.
I wasn't dead was my first clue to my whereabouts, I was cold
was my second, lastly I was starving and in pain. Five or six feet
from me was a fire and something that smelled like food.

  I attempted to gain my feet but was turned away, so I decided
that crawling would have to suffice. Meat sizzled above the
fire on a stick and water was in a deep polished rock beside.

  Stars filled the sky over sand as far I as could see and there was

178

SHANE

still no life anywhere. Further, I was alive and had eaten the meat, drank the water and was resting. Puzzled at the turn of events I called to Truth but he did not answer my summons.

Justice, come to me son.

 The silence was unbroken once more.

DAMN!!! What the hell am I supposed to do now?

 No answer was to come and once more I was in the grip of exhaustion.

I slept.

 I awoke to the sun rising over the land, sitting up I noticed that there was no trace of the fire not even coals. Earlier in my journeys I might have this strange but not now.

 I walked in the direction of the sun for hours, seeing nothing but the sun to beckon me onward. I wondered around in that frying pan for weeks seeing nothing, yet every night I had meat to eat and water to drink. I never realized what having another soul to be with meant to me before there was none. Hours turned to days, days to weeks, weeks to months and still there was nothing.

 Night fell as it has since creation and the food was their only this time I didn't eat it or drink the water. I figured why eat and drink just to live a few days longer, no that was it I lost

179

SHANE

hope and in my **SOLITUDE** I chose to let my fate have me.

 Morning reared it's head again, but this time I saw a structure in the distance. It was at least a days hard march but it was there and I felt renewed. Near nightfall I reached the structure, tired beyond normal human limits, yet I was here.

 I noticed a pool of water in the corner, so I stumbled over to it to drink. Kneeling to drink I saw an old face with long whitish whiskers in the pool. Has it been so long that I am reduced to an old man to die alone and empty. No way in hell am I going to go to my reward on my knees like a coward in failure. If there is an in, then there is a way out, I will have to find it.
 Pretending to be asleep I waited to see where the fire and the food came from. A small lithe figure set the fire burning and placed the meat on the stick noticing that I had a pool of water it turned right into me.

 I seize it's arm and said be still you are in no danger.

 We walked over to the fire so I could get a better look at the person who had feed me and kept me alive.

 What are you I said to the person.

 Before me was a small girl covered in fine red hair with pointed ears and crystal blues eyes that blink out at me. I am Havax, and I kept you alive because I felt sorry for you, she said in a soft silk voice.

SHANE

Why the hell didn't you show yourself to me before this, I said?

I am small and you could have made me your prisoner, or worse eat me.

I wouldn't eat you, your the only person that I have seen since coming here.

We talked all night and part of the day since we had shelter and water. Havax told me that there were others there like her but they usually killed strangers for food, so she steered me away from any of them.

Why didn't you do me in while I slept?

She smiled and said, you interest me, I have never seen anything like you before and I wanted to know what happened to your ears and hair. Then, your hair started growing in a way I have never seen.

My beard you mean, I said? Do you have something sharp, a knife or something?

Havax produced a razor sharp knife from an calf sheath and handed it to me.

Wonder was written all over my new friend face when I shaved my face. I elected not to cut my long hair but to braid it instead. Havax stood up (four and a half feet tall at best) and

181

SHANE

walked over to me, then ran her hands over my face.

She smiled and said, your beautiful.

I said, I would be more beautiful if I was clean.

What is clean asked Havax?

It is where you clean your body after you remove any garments that you wear with water and soap if you have it.

Show me this clean, she said. I can't the only water we have is in the pool and we need that to drink.

Havax looked at the pool and said, that pool is fifty feet wide and five times as deep where it meets the underground sea.

Upon hearing her explanation of how the water table worked I said, ok lets get wet babs.

What is babs, asked Havax?

It is a way of saying friend Havax.

I took off my clothing and drove into the pool, which I should have done before, because it felt so good.

When I came up Havax said, your face is changed.

SHANE

What do you mean?

The lines that were there now are not.

 Really, well perhaps the lines were cause by the dirt.

No, your hair is no longer white either.

In that case this is what I look like as a young man.

She asked, what is young?

 It is when you have not lived a long time, you know before you get old.

 What is getting old, Havax asked?

 Being old is having lines on your face that don't go away, your hair becomes grey and parts of your body don't work as well as when you were young.

How old are you Sean asked Havax?

 I thought for a moment, then replied forty eight I guess, you see I have been traveling though many portals and time has been lost for me at this point.

 How old are you honey?

 I have seen the rains come and go eighty three times.

SHANE

Your eighty-three, I said!

Yes, barely more than a child I know Havax said.

Well, how old do you people live to be?

Many hundreds of cycles or until they are killed or die in the desert looking for food.

Upon finishing the discussion on age, I persuaded Havax to join me in the water. Havax knelt and removed her knife from her leg, then she stood up and started fiddling with her neck. Suddenly a small sleek little bra shaped thing was pulled away from her breasts, which I didn't notice before. Further, she pulled the same sort of sleek invisible garment away from her crotch. She stood there in the light from the window naked for the first time.

I had earlier thought that she was young and undeveloped, I now knew that the garments that she wore were restrictive. Before me stood a small athletically built naked young woman. Her breast were pert and much larger than they looked when she was clothed(I didn't even see any clothing before she removed them) and the rest of her finely toned body was very appealing to look at especially since I been alone for such a long time. She smiled at me shyly then took a couple of steps and jumped into the water, coming right up in front of me by only an inch or so.

The water was cold in the pool and the air was hot so it made a

184

match as Havax and I played in the water like children, although we both felt the animal attraction between us. As we were wrestling around we were playfully fondling each others naked bodies. Havax seemed to enjoy the wave of attention I was giving her and she responded by returning the affection I was showing her. On a rock in the shallow water near the shore of the pool I sat down. Havax was walking on the bottom when I sat because she could hold her breath a long time underwater. She popped up after several minutes with a gasp for air turned and swam over to me.

What are you doing Sean, she asked?

I am just sitting here looking at you and thinking about . . .

She smiled and said what?

I reached into the water and picked her out of it, holding her to my chest I kissed her.

Long moments went by unnoticed while I held her to the embrace. When I pulled my lips from hers she looked shocked and a little scared. In fact she was shaking in my arms.

What's the matter Havax, I said?

She looked up and said I did not think I would be doing anything like this for several years to come and I am afraid.

I held her close to me and said If You're not ready to give that

185

SHANE

kind of relationship, that's ok there's no hurry, I'm not going anywhere.

Looking into my eyes she tried to say something but the words would not come to life in her mouth, so I said I know.

She held me tightly against her body and I could feel her hard little nipples pressing against my chest. We moved away from the water and laid down, still holding each other until slumber came.

In a deep sleep I dreamed of a place high above a spinning galaxy where I sat with Truth and talked of how we would take care of the governing of it.

Elsewhere, Justin appeared in front of Jeanie and said LOVE YA BABE! Jeanie was laying on her bed looking at the ceiling.

She jumped off the bed into his arms and said, Where hell have you been? Before he was able to answer she kissed him as a woman dying and this was her last chance. The embrace lasted for ten minutes before she let him up for air.

I missed you too Jeanie, Justin said.

Where is Bob and Sean Justin, Jeanie wanted to know?

Truth is in council with the Almighty, and Destiny my father is on a quest to find his inner strength because he is going to need it when he faces the one with a dark motive.

186

SHANE

How is Nicky, he asked Jeanie?

How do you think with Sean gone to God knows where, said Jean.

Tell me where your quest has taken you lover boy, Jeanie said as she grabbed Justin and pushed him on the bed.

Hours of intense lovemaking were to come before the tale that Justin would spin in perfect detail. However, the was no hurry as far as Justin could see, enjoying the moment seemed paramount at this time.

When I opened my eyes the day had already ended and night covered the land. I looked around and did not see Havax anywhere, I thought that she probably left to go home. A noise behind me and to the left alerted me to the fact I was not alone after all. I grabbed a rock from the ground and took a defensive posture, just incase it was not a friend visitor I faced in the dark.

Havax came into the moonbeam and said, are you going to hit me with that rock?

I looked at the rock in my hand and dropped it, no I don't think so.

That's good, she said, because I caught us some food to eat since we slept all day.

SHANE

We supped hard on the animal she brought, then we went over
and curled up on the pile of cloth we slept on together. We sleep.
The morning came to the sound feet outside of our shelter. I
began to get up but Havax put her arms around me and rolled
over on me, just act like we are mating and they won't pay us
any attention.

She was sadly mistaken. They made a beeline for us.

 One of them said, so Havax you reach adulthood good, we shall
all enjoy you after this wonderer.

I think not, I said.   Havax said, he is not a wanderer, he is my
mate.

 They laughed and said then we challenge him for you Havax.

 I said, do I have to answer this challenge or can it be ignored.

The one who spoke before said, he is to cowardly to even fight
for his woman.

At that I sprang to my feet, my teeth clinched and my eyes red
and narrow with anger. The sight of my greater size and
hairlessness scared the shit out of them momentarily.

You want to fight, so be it, I said.

 I kicked him in the face, spun and swept his companions feet
out from under them. They hit the ground hard with a thud, yet

188

SHANE

they regained there feet quickly as a well trained warrior would.
They circled me spear or knife in hand which ever they had,
ready to spring the moment I focused on one of them. I knew
their strategy was to distract me while one of the others
stabbed me, so I didn't focus on anyone of them until they were
in striking range then I hit them so damn hard that they were
coughing up blood.

 However, I had to admire their bravery at fighting on in the face
of sure death. A sharp pain in back brought my attention back to
the matters at hand. My break in concentration cost me a
vicious stab wound in my back on the left side. I leaned forward
quickly removing the knife from my back, I caught his arm at the
wrist and turn on him with bloodlust for revenge. It was granted,
he would see home no more.

 His two friend were very afraid now because I had caused them
moral wounds bare handed and now I had a knife. They let out a
cry then rushed me.   I deflected the attackers spear on my right
and buried my knife in the chest of my opponent on the left
which fell dead at my feet. His loud mouthed partner turned and
tried to flee, but I threw the knife and it found it's home in his
right upper leg.

 He tried to stab me but I grabbed his spear and said, take your
dead friend with you pal and don't ever come here again or I will
kill you too.

I took the spear and the knife I stuck in him away and told him to
go once I tied both of his dead comrades to him, so he would

189

SHANE

remember and anyone he ran into would remember that picking
a fight can be a deadly business if you underestimate your
target.. He left dragging his buddies behind him, leaving a trail of
blood that would attract predators. It is the Indian in
me that made me want to punish my foe in the way as they would
have in my place.

 The blood from the fight was all over and I had lost more blood
than any other, yet I was still up on my feet. Suddenly, without
any warning it hit, the pain from the stab wound and weakness in
my knees as the world began to spin and the darkness. I fell and
finally blacked out.

 Havax was tending to my rather extensive wounds when I was
able to detect my surroundings, though it was though a slight
fog.

 How are you, asked Havax?

 I feel like shit, how are you?

I am well, but you're in a serious way, she said tears fell.

 What do you mean, I asked?

 Their weapons are dipped into poison so that if they only wound
an animal they can track it until it dies.

 Death, not my first choice, is there an alternative Babe?

190

SHANE

 YES, but it is painful, you might die anyway, said the red haired beauty.

Hell, I am sure as shoot going to die if we don't try it! What do we do, I asked?

 You need not do anything, she said sadly, I however will do what I can.

 The circle of stones was nearly finished when Havax began to chant in a tongue I didn't know. Tears were still falling from her eyes, yet she carried on without falter. A strange sensation began to come slowly over me. A light fog fell over our dwelling. The ceremony went on for several more hours.

Havax was starting to glow just before dawn when she said, This gift I give to you willingly.

The glow around her intensified and began around me when I suddenly realized what the gift was she was giving me. HER LIFE!!

With a burst of flame from my eyes I rose from the ground where I was laying.

No, dear little Havax you will not give your life for me!

 However, she already gave me her life-force and lying on the ground by the fire unmoving.

SHANE

I walked over to her, knelt, looked at the stars and said, I know I said I was not going to ever interfere with the life/death balance, but I ask that just this once you allow me this little life that was giving so freely for my own.

My whole body glowed so bright white that ever the sun was dull in comparison. I reached right into heaven where the hand of GOD touched mine and gave me Havax's soul with his divine blessing.

I gave my thanks humbly and returned Havax to her body.

Meanwhile, Jeanie sat in total awe as Justice spun the tale of his travels through the cosmos. You cannot imagine what it feels like to feel the power to reach out and touch the stars at will and have them talk back to you in language that you hear all the time, but only now can understand.

Yet, I feel sorry for dad.

Why ask Jen.

Well, Jen he is by far the most powerful of all the guardians of the universe, and he is the chosen one, but doesn't know it. He can never die, Jeanie, he is going to live forever. What about you lover, said Jen?

I will live a hell of a long time but sooner or later I will choose a successor to take my place, and I will retire.

SHANE

Will you die then, asked
Jeanie?

  No, then I start to age very slowly and eventually die, Justin
explained.

 Will you still have your powers she asked?

Yeah, Till the day I die then the knew JUSTICE will be at full
power and fully trained in his duties.

What about me Justin, where will I be while your running all over
the damned place?

 With me silly, where the hell did you think, asked Justin with a
twisted little smile.

   Justin sat on a chair in the corner of the galley where we
usually eat and said let me start at the beginning. After dad left
Goth asked me to walk with him, do you remember Jen?

Yeah, I remember that she said to Justin.

 He told me that there are four keys that work together and the
master key that binds them all. Destiny, is my father and Truth is
Bob, and he asked me to take up the mantle of the living justice.
I accepted and became Justice once I took the key that bore my
symbol. Lost in a valley of giants the moment I touched the
damn thing, I didn't yet realize that the key was not the power of
Justice but I myself was. I wandered through the jungle at my

SHANE

ever side looking for any sign of life. Life found me in only minutes after I started looking for help or just someone to tell me what or where I was. It was a rat wearing a hat, gloves, shirt and pants all of green.

Hi, I said in the hopes that he was not a mean hungry bastard looking for a meal, because he was at least twice my height and ten times my weight.

Hi yerself mate, he said looking at my expression at his words. Are ya dangerous mate or are ya a friend I haven't met yet?

We stood there looking at each other for several minutes before a word more was spoken.

You sound Australian friend, are you, said Justin to the giant rat?

What's an Australian mate, he said to me said Justin.

It is someone who talks like you, I said to the rat explained Justin.

Hell all Rat folk speak this away, and why are ya walking around hee fo, said the rat?

I am lost and don't have a clue as to where I am, I said to the rat.

Well, I am gunna help ya mate said the rat. I'm Roden, he said

SHANE

holding out his hand to me for a shake.

I shook it, explained Justin, We were about to go when I said,
wait I almost forgot I have to help find the master key of time
and space.

A big job mate, one that will require some help eh. Come on he
said with a wink.

I knew that he was truly going to be my friend at that point.
The journey took two hour hours and Roden told me much about
the jungle as we traveled, yet he was holding something back.
The jungle rose up as we approached a fortress that would have
pleased MacArthur at that engineering and structure. It was
truly a sight to behold, with wall thicker than fort Knox and
battlements full of guards, it was the mystical immovable object.
Roden must have noticed the silly look on my face because he
started chuckling and patted me on the back.

I don't think anything could knock down the walls of it. Ten
minutes later we stood at the vast structure, but there was no
visible gate to enter. Roden placed his hand on the wall and a
huge door opened to admit us. WE entered the fort and it was
incredible inside, with statues as tall as buildings of everything
from trees to mice. Roden bid me follow him, so I did and the
sights were great and I told him so. Great pillars loomed down
from the building that we were entering. The floors were made of
gold and the walls of jade.

Your people must be very rich to build buildings like this

SHANE

Roden, I said.

Yeeh, we got sum grand stuff round hee, said Roden.

In a room with some very old rats we stopped and asked
permission to enter.   A red rat came out looked at me and said,
were did you get the new pet Roden?

I am not a pet asshole, yelled Justin.

What it can speak, but that's not possible, where did it come
from Roden ,asked the red rat?

Justin came from another world and he got the key of bloomin
Justice on'm, Roden explained..

Show me slave, said the big loud mouth rat.

Roden grabbed his arm and said, he is hee as ma mate so geet
off'm. With that said Roden gave red a good shove. Go announce
us boot leeker before I put me boots in your backside!

The door opened and all eyes where trained squarely on the key
that hung around my neck, Justin told Jen.

A wave of mummers erupted from the old rats that were seated
until one very ancient rat held up his hand, then you could
hear dust fall on the floor.

Where did you get the key around your neck lil fella, said the very

196

SHANE

old rat?

 Goth, the keeper gave it to me so I could enter the battle to come as Justice.

 Many whispered their disbelief in my tale, but the oldest rat said be still or leave to the assembly and it was quiet again.

If your telling truth then use your powers lil thing with no tail, said t he old rat.

He would regret that request.

 I took the key from my neck and said, IN ALL THINGS THERE WILL BE JUSTICE!

I felt the power rage through me like lightning and I realized that I was floating ten feet off the ground and blue fire made the symbol of Justice in front of me, Justin explained.

 All were shaking in fear, yet the old rat and Roden stood up unafraid.

 Roden said, I guess I made a good and powerful decision today to be your best mate.

 The old rat said, it is true you are truly the living Justice.

 The red rat jumped up and grabbed the key from around my neck and said now I have the power.

197

SHANE

Roden laughed then said luk bahind ya-sef mate.

Red turned and found me unmoved and kinda mad to boot.

So you want power eh, okay here it is, said Justice.

Red rat got hit by one blue lightning bolt from the tip of my
finger and his hair stood straight up and he was thrown clear
across the tremendously big room, hitting the wall to stop him. I
set back down onto the floor and stopped glowing.

Will that do as a show of force old one, Justice said?

Yeeh, I think it otta do Master Justice, besides me fur issa
standin op rught now.

Justin said, I didn't know I could do that before now.

Well I hope it won't be necessary again, said the old rat. I am
Nutm, leader of all the Rat folk and we are honored that your
here he said.

Bullshit, you wished I never came, said Justin.

How did you know that, said Nutm?

I told him said the voice in the air.

SHANE

Show yourself then, if your gonna interject you should join us, Nutm said.

Very well, a figure faded into view in front of Nutm.

An who are ya then said Nutm?

I am Truth, and I know all.

The assembly hall was quickly full of guards who were all pointing there weapons at Truth.

Red yelled kill them all now before they can geet away.

The guards obeyed but I placed a protective Shield around Roden just incase, Truth just laughed as the guards ran right through him. I started laughing when their spears and swords just broke when they hit me.

Truth, said Justin, by the way as key masters we are invulnerable to harm as you know it.

Nutm stood and said, stop this foolishness guards and get out. As for you red rat your seat on the assembly is forfeit for bad mannas and stupidity, now get out! Justice made his first enemy that day Justin explained to Jeanie as she curled up on his lap.

Back in the wastelands, Havax opened her eyes and said, how's this possible, I should be dead. I remember the creator saying that it was good for me to come back to someone but I couldn't

SHANE

see them. Whoever, it was must be very powerful for GOD to grant such a favor, said Havax. She turned and looked at me, froze in fear at the sight of me.

 Yes, it was I who brought you back, but I let to much of my pure essence out and I still have not totally regain control. What she saw was me glowing like a small sun and my eyes were bright red and I was floating above the ground. Come to me Havax, there is no danger.

 She got up and walked over to me, then said I understand because my soul and yours were together as one for a moment and I know all that you feel and think, she said. One thing more your mingling with me has given you the ability to cure by a simply touch and other things, I started to tell Havax.

I never finished because she pressed her tiny lips to mine and said, I love you and you know that, as I know the tears of life that you shed for me in the Face of GOD to regain my soul....

Truly for all my power, I was on my knees crying and begging GOD to allow me the one boon, I vow to never perform, and was granted that gift if only once. Hers was not a life that should be spent on my account. Her purpose was not fulfilled yet.

 We floated in the air for a long time just holding each other because that seemed to be what the moment called for. Morning came to the sound of Havax little lips kissing my neck.

 We are not floating anymore, I said.

200

SHANE

We must have made a soft landing in our sleep, added Havax.
WE should go to my people now and tell them that they have a
healer now.

I guess it wouldn't hurt, I said.

Your eyes are still glowing red Sean, she pointed out.

I thought for a moment, then I closed my eyes and made them go
back to normal. How's that I asked Havax?

Better, but how are we going to get to my village without food
or water she asked.

Come outside and I'll show you.

The sun bleach sand look like a sea to us as the wind blew it
around.

Watch, I said to her as I knelt placing my hand in the sand up to
my wrist.

Havax was right at my shoulder peering down for some hidden
result when I started to glow a greenish hue and the sand
turned wet, then to soil and suddenly little green plants
sprang up from within the moist earth.

I turned to Havax and said where is your village? She pointed to
our south, I shook my head and smiled then with a burst of

201

SHANE

energy that she felt, plants sprang up in rows heading for her home.

 A miracle, she asked?

You know better than that love, I said to her. I am doing it so this place isn't dead all over, I said.

Why did you choose those plants, she asked me?

 I reached over her shoulder and said, see for yourself as I grabbed something then handed it to her.

It is a fruit of some kind, isn't it she said biting into it?

 Yes and every plant bares a different fruit than the one before and after it, I said. They will be all the food and drink will shall require along the way.

 The journey began only minutes after I showed Havax the fruit trees that I planted because we had nothing to take with us. We walked for days and nights seeing nobody but we talked and laughed as truly happy people did.

Finally, the night was broken by a joyous shout from our south. We got up and walked towards the shouting to find out what was happening. There were eleven of Havax's race celebrating at finding the fruit trees. One seen us coming and alerted the others.

SHANE

What do you want here strangers, asked a short wiry man with anger in his voice?

We heard your laughter and shouts and came to see why you were so happy.

We have found these fruit plants and are happy we will not starve.

I am glad that my trees will help you and yours survive friend, I said.

These are our trees stranger not yours, he said rudely!! GO AWAY NOW, he shouted.

You don't understand friend I don't want your food, I planted these trees so that people like you would find them and eat.

He is trying to trick us, I say we kill him now.

What the hell is wrong with you, he made these trees to feed our people and your talking of fighting over them, said Havax.

After we finish with the stranger your next girl, said the man who did most of the talking.

We all stood there looking at each other in the faint moonlight, waiting for what was to come next.

The waiting did not take long. The thin man who was for killing

203

SHANE

us first threw his spear at Havax. I was going to step over and
catch it but, Havax turned it away with a wave of her hand. A
small boy was struck with the spear, which I remembered were
dipped in poison. The boy fell to the ground and his father said,
son what is it. He ran over to the boy and fell to his knees
beside the fallen youth, and the rest of his party attacked. I
raised my hand and fire burst from my hand into the dark night
sky illuminating the shallow valley where we all stood.

   ENOUGH, I said in a thunderous voice that shook the ground
and made the attackers stop in the tracks and shake with fear.

   The boy needs help the father said to the leader of the party.

He turned to me and Havax. Can you help my son, he begged?

Havax walked over to the father and said, have no fear your son
will be just fine in a moment.

   She knelt down over the boy and touched his wound and said be
not afraid boy your in no danger now I have healed you. The boy
looked a little afraid in spite of Havax's soothing words. Yet, he
stood up and hugged his father, I'm not dead father she has
made me well!

The leader of the party knelt in-front of Havax and said, your a
angel aren't you.

   No, I am not but I am able to heal anything that is living as long
as it wants my help.   The rest of the party was on there knees as
204

SHANE

well bowing to Havax.

Then all of a sudden they remembered me behind them and they turned in time to see the boy walk over to me and say, doesn't that fire burn you?

 No, it is not really fire but the light from my soul manifesting in the form of fire so you could comprehend it.

 How do you do it, make the light shine through I mean, said the boy?

 I have very special abilities that make me able to control the forces that every person has within them but never lets out because they don't know how.

The party all had their faces in the sand for fear that I was going to destroy them I thought, but not the boy he was way to fascinated by the magik in the air.

I said get up people, your not my servants and I am not a king or a god although my powers are greater than any god you could think of other than the creator, my LORD GOD.

 WE took the people to our camp and told them of our quest to find Havax's village and to bring prosperity back to the land, and that is why I planted the fruit trees in rows in the desert to feed hungry travelers.

 The boy was asleep in my lap as his father told me that there

SHANE

were few villages that were not under the heel of the desert ruler at this time and Havax's home was sure to be conquered by now if was much farther south.

It was getting late so all of us decided that we would work on our problems in the morning.

It was just after midnight when the father woke my sleepy ass up and said, Sean we are all lost if we don't find some shelter fast.

Why I asked in a yawning way? There is a major sand blizzard coming this way, he retorted.

I looked around and said, I don't see a thing.

True there is nothing as of yet but I know these things and I am afraid for us, said the farther.

Okay, I said. Give me that rock I said, while I was getting to my feet.

He gave it to me and I rolled it over and over in my hand, then I said little brother stone we ask you for your protection this night, will you become a mighty boulder to save us?

The others all looked at me as if I were insane, why would I talk to a rock when we might be killed by the coming storm, except Havax who knew I was Destiny and could do things that they didn't understand.

206

SHANE

The small stone seemed to be humming in my hand, all of a sudden it said give it to my baby, make me what I can be, let me serve you who serve us all.

The people were afraid at the revelation that the stone was alive and could speak.

I raise my eyes to the sky and said, so be it then, the choose has been made and I through up the stone.   The sky ten feet above us is as high as the stone went. It burst into many different shapes and sizes. The air also was changing, into different colors as the tiny stone became a great rock fortress over us.

The fortress in a humming voice said, it is done and all who enter here shall be protected.   Then he voice was gone.

I laid back down and Havax came over and curled up with me to go to sleep again.

How can you sleep said the leader of the party, how do you know that this place can hold up to the storm?

Did you not just hear the dome say he swore us protection as long as we are in here, I said?

Yes, but how can a stone become a fortress, his walls must be thin and weak, said the leader.

SHANE

Dome open the wall so we can exit please, I asked.

The wall opened where there were no doors or even cracks.

Come here all of you, I said, look at his walls.

 They all came outside and looked at the might structure that was our fort.

 All of this from a single small stone said the boy, wow!

His father said, yes it is very grand, but look over there and he pointed to our far eastern side.

The sight of the unstoppable juggernaut was one that even made me doubt the fortress but I said we should be safely inside before to long folks or we are going to get a free sandblasting.

 However, not even I could bring myself to stop looking at the storm coming, yet it approached at a terrible rate. The fortress saw that the storm would over take us at any second extended his walls around us pulling us in hard and fast just as the storm crashed into dome our protector.

 There was no sound of the tempest raging outside from within domes walls. A faint face in the wall seemed to smile at the victory of saving us from the death winds outside and the boy saw the face.

Are you the face of the dome, he said while he touched the wall?

SHANE

The face only nodded it's head but did not speak because it was using it's magik to protect us at the moment. So, speech was not advisable.

Morning came to the sound of dome explaining to the desert people who I was and that my power is literally without limit but I did not like to let it out because of it's terrible strength. Havax joined in by telling of the way she came to be able to heal and protect herself magikly.

The desert people looked at me very differently then on, it was with respect and pity, I believed because of my mammoth task that laid ahead. We all went out to see what the windstorm had done to the land. The sun was still low in the sky when we stepped outside and froze in total astonishment at the grizzly sight we beheld. The ground as far as the eye could see in any direction was devoid of sand. Rocks and dirt were all that remained and they were a hundred feet below where we now stood. Dome's foundation went all the way to the rocks far below. He must have sensed that we wanted to go down for a look because the rock face blurred and came back into sharp focus with large steps going all the way to the valley floor.

Good show dome, I said as I led the way down the steps.

Flat as a dollar bill was the valley floor in every direction. All that stood tall and defiant was dome who was polished like a mirror as were all the rocks from the mad whirlwind. I thought for a moment that dome was going to be made a sacred place

SHANE

because he is magik and therefore special.

Well what now folks, I asked them?

We need to find some food to eat or we'll starve, said the leader.

I said does anyone have any food left on them from yesterday?

I do said the leaders woman, but it is not enough for even me and we have no water!

Before I could answer the woman Havax bent down and put her hand flat against the ground and said, let me heal you so that you may sustain us on our journey mother earth.

The leader said, now Havax thinks that she is a demigod like Sean.

However, he was already choking on his words before Havax turned to him, because water sprang up out of the rocks where her hand was. We shall drink on our journey, she said with a twisted little smile at me.

The food was still in question when I said, give me all the food that everyone has.

Why, so you can eat it while we starve said a woman?

I am not mortal miss I do not need food to live like you do.

SHANE

  The Boy grabbed the food and placed it on a flat piece of rock in the center of us all, then looked at me and said, go ahead Sean do it.

I smiled at his quick understanding of my plan. Okay, you got it I said. Stand back so your not in the firing line of this, I said. I raised my hands and said, we're hungry so grow to feed us, then I started glowing greenish and I pointed at the food which grew. The boy was the first to cheer, even the woman had to admit my plan had worked out swimmingly.

SHANE

SHANE

CHAPTER EIGHT: A NEW LAND.

A week after we left dome we walked on toward the southern home of my new mate Havax. The land was all dry and seemed dead but wherever Havax touched the ground, and a hundred yard circle of life began to grow and water always came up in the hollows of rock depressions which made great lil swimming pools in the hot dusty desert land we were in.

The desert people that were traveling with us started to call Havax the Shama, which is the female version of a shaman and in her peoples culture is the highest of titles and carries great honor with it whether it is because you can heal or not. Havax was very pleased at the development though she tried not to let it show, which amused me.

The journey was hard on the desert people and I had not realized how until the father dropped on his face from exhaustion.

Havax I never considered that you are superhuman now that you were joined with me and I am an eternal and don't get tired but our friend are all burnt out and need to be rested for many days to be able to go on, I said.

She thought for a moment and said, your right I have not been tired since I was join with you and our companions are suffering

SHANE

from heat stroke and I didn't notice. Why didn't any of you say something, Havax asked them?

 You are the Shama and Sean is a god as we have seen, we though you would leave us behind if we said anything about it to you. You are both to great to be bothered with our little problems, said the leader.

I had tears rolling down my cheeks after I heard his testimony. You are without a doubt a great man, you thought of your people before yourself and it breaks my heart that you thought we not help you to survive. I am not a God thought a very gift man, with God giving grace yes, but I am not a God, just a special man.

 I walked away from them right over the rocks and out of sight followed by Havax who knew my thoughts and was pleased. The desert people to weak to follow us thought that we were leaving them behind and Started to beg for help, but we kept going anyway.

 The leader said to his people it is my fault that we are here because I told him why we would not speak and he and The Shama were insulted and they left us because we are not worthy of their help.

I was just out of their sight where they would be in no danger at what I had to do.

 I said to Havax protect yourself as I blasted a hole in the rocks a hundred feet deep and three hundred wide, then I gave way as

SHANE

Havax stepped up glowing as red as I was. She said nothing but set right to the task which was bigger than she knew, filling the small lake with the water of life, a water that never can get dirty or polluted. Havax walked into the dry lake I had just made and began to cast forth in search for the water of life. The water sprang forth from the bottom of the lake but it was not enough for the purpose we had in mind. Although Havax was superhuman this task was putting a fantastic strain on her.

I don't have enough strength to do this Sean.

I said, are you ready.

She said for what? A beam of pure energy hit her surrounding her hole body in the light of ten thousand sun going nova at once. She screamed in pain, then in ecstasy from the unimaginable power that she was directing to the purpose that she alone chose. She knew at once the Gift of God's embrace and the joy of her own Destiny.

The water rushed into the lake and splashed up on her feet and she smiled through glowing eyes. The power feels goods, but it was you who made me able to complete the lake of life, said Havax.

I only made the energy available for you to finish your job, I told her Why am I still glowing, it was your magik that I was using?

Not anymore, the energy I fed you was absorbed by you, so you have it in reserve from now on, I explain.

SHANE

The desert people were scared by the awesome force of our new creation and when we came over the rocks back where they were, the fact that we were glowing bright red did not help to calm them.

O God help us we're going to die, said the leader.

No your not I said, I'm still glowing from unleashing my energies in vast quantities.

Shama your glowing to said a woman. I was energized with power beyond reason and now I have it within me, because of Sean, he gave it to me for you.

Yes but where did he get it from, asked the Father of the boy?

GOD All mighty, I said, the creator of us all.

I started carrying the boy and his father to the lake.
Havax picked up the leader who was twice her size and started toward the lake also.

How is it that you can carry me so easily, your muscle are not even flexing?

I am twenty time more strong than anyone in the land save Sean himself who is at least five thousand times as strong, said Havax.

Incredible, yet I believe it, said the leader.

216

SHANE

We carried all the people to the lake and put them in. At once all of them were totally rejuvenated and ready to go on, but we said no we should stay so you can supercharge your system with the life waters.

A full week passed before we even started to get ready to leave. It took that long for Havax to stop glowing and come under control of her new might. I never told her that her powers would only work for the good of or health of something and not to destroy. However I saw no evil in her and loved her very much although I missed Nicky terribly allot of the time.

Then came the night that leaving was right, so we gathered up all the water that the desert people could carry, which was allot now that they had the water of life in them. We set forth to the south once more in search of Havax people. Twenty days passed happily with everyone in good spirits and in excellent health. A small structure was set off in the distance ahead of us, so we made a beeline for it in the hope that we would find someone there who would have news of Havax's village.

The father touched my arm as we approached and said, there is great evil here and I think danger for even you Sean.

Are you psychic, father asked his son?

Yes, if you mean can I see the future events, I say we be cautious in this matter.

217

SHANE

What do you think, leader, I asked?

Father is never wrong, so we are in danger, I think Caution is a good word for us I say.

WE went forth carefully, just incase of big trouble. The road was well travel we all noticed as we drew near that was a clue that there may be a bunch of them laying in the weeds for us if you know what I mean. The house was not that small when our party closed on it from the northwest side where there were few tracks to show a foe waiting for us.

An eerie feeling fell over the place surrounding the house and the sky even seemed to dull. All at once the horde that awaited us, emerged. They were desert folk but as big as me and they had a strange aura about they. I noticed movement from the rear of the crowd that were staring at us with steely eyes.

Thy presence here pleases me stranger, said a figure holding a glowing orb.

Why is that, I replied?

Because I can feel your power my friend and Frankly I want that power, he said with a menacing grin.

First I must know who you are, I said to him with a twist smile?

He regarded me slowly after I asked that question.

SHANE

I believe it was because I was smiling very wildly like a crazy man in a toy store. His weight shifted from foot to foot and he began to nervously finger the glowing ball. My icy stare, in combination with the strange grin, pretty much unhorse the dirty little evil sprite in front of me. I could tell that he was up to no good and that is just, what he was up to, this meant that he must be dealt with before we can go on.

I said, there is great evil here and I think you Are psychic, father.

The ugly evil bug-eyed man took two steps toward me and stopped regarding me carefully.

I am Zer the ruler of the desert, Who are you, asked Zer?

I am Sean, and what makes you think I have any sort of power or energy about me, I responded?

He didn't have to tell me that, I already knew because he held the Orb of Tarshi, which is the stealer of souls.

My little ball talks to me and it told me that you were so powerful that I must let the ball drink of your energy, said Zer.

Is that right, I scoffed.

Yes, it is, said Zer.

SHANE

Fool, it is the Orb of Tarshi that you hold and it is drinking your soul a little at a time so it can control you, I yelled at him.

You are going to die for that insult stranger, shrieked a mad Zer.

The gauntlet was thrown into the ring and one us must die to mend the balance here in the desert. Zer backed off to a spot where none of his storm troopers were at risk from the come hurricane of death that would no doubt result.

I told Havax you have the power to shield yourself from any attack, even from the power of the orb and your must keep the desert people who are our friends safe to in an cloak of invisibility.

She said, what about you Sean?

Never mind me just get the hell out of here with our party and I shall deal with this madman!

I meandered to the place where Zer was waiting for me with hollow eyes of despair and lust for power that he was never to experience through the death orb. I stone faced Zer, pondering the numerous times I had faced my own death and the destruction of the known universe. It seemed funny that I, just a little boy from Ridgefield would end up the champion of it all, the protector of the weak and thousands of races that I still hadn't seen.

Meanwhile, Justin finished his tale for Jeanie and Nicky

220

SHANE

had been listening on for any news of me, when Bob (Truth)
materialized right next to Nicky. She jumped and hit him, you
crazy bastard, ya scared the hell out of me!

Justin said, ho bro what do ya know?

I know that there is love in your hearts, he said pointing
at Justin and Jeanie. Yet, this one is dreadfully sad over the lost
love she yearns for, he said placing his hand on Nicky's Shoulder.

I wish I could see him again, said Nicky as she started to cry.

Done, said Truth to Nicky!

Bob walked over and grabbed a mammoth pan from the wall and
took it to the sink put water in it, then said come her all
of you. Bob put his hand in the water and said show me the
truth. Bob began to glow very bright white the so did the water.
Justin said, don't be afraid it is just a side effect of being
nearly all-powerful.

The water started to take a shape and a color that was
familiar to them, namely me. They saw me walking out on the
field of battle, then it seemed as the water panned back to show
the whole field of view.

That's when Justin said, o'my God isn't that the Orb of Tarshi,
Bob?

Yes, that is it, he responded.

221

SHANE

Can that thing beat Destiny's unmatchable might in combat, Truth? At the question Bob was transformed into the living truth, a creature of pure energy that is knowledge.

Perhaps in the right hands Justice. Justin transmutated into Justice and stood there glowing a rich blue color.

Jeanie said, wow that's some getup baby, I like it.

He didn't answer her, Instead his eyes were glued to the watery images unfold.

There was no sounds as we faced off twenty yards apart in the midday sunshine. Zer was looking a little unsteady as he raised the orb in front of himself and spoke the words even though he did not know there meaning.

Orb of power grant me this day the might to vanquish your enemies and drink their souls in greater glory, shouted Zer.

A beam of intense magnitude hit me in the chest throwing me sixty feet, yet it was not intended to absorb my energies, but to soften me up I guessed.

I just got up and started laughing at Zer, your going to have do a sight better than that if your going to defeat me insect.

Yes, that is it, like an insect, I said to the confusion of all who watched except Truth who I was not aware of it.

SHANE

The crowd gasped and drew back when I started to glow green all over. Justice told Jeanie put on your sunglasses or look away because dad is about to unleash his power and it is a terrifying sight even to me and I am nearly as all powerful as dad.

Truth waved his hand and sunglasses that were glowing appeared in his hands and he gave them to Nicky and Jeanie.

Floating forty above the ground I began to grow until my feet were flat on the ground again. Zer was shaking in fear at the sight of my now forty foot stature.

I will defeat you still your size means nothing to the orb, said Zer.

He was correct, yet he did not know whom he was facing, nor I would bet did the orb. Zer held up the orb and another fantastic beam emerged. I knew it was coming so I just directed it back on the sender. Zer knew the truth all in the second that the beam hit him, then with a cry for help he was gone. However, the orb was still there floating in the air where Zer had just stood a few seconds before.

In a voice that was thousands of voices in one the orb said, I now know who you are Lord Destiny but that will not save you from being absorbed.

Another beam shot out at the crowd and I reached over and let it hit my hand.

223

SHANE

The orb cried with ecstasy as the power of my hand was being absorbed, see I told you that I would have you, exclaimed the ball of death.

You want me then, have me you son-of-a-bitch!

I let all my power go all at once totally leaving the shell that was my invincible body, to a pure form of raw might.

Nicky cried, help him that ball is killing my Sean!!

I am sorry but no one may help him now, besides he is ten times more powerful than either of us, said Truth.

Justin said, nothing short of God himself could take Destiny out, and God loves him, so **TAKE HEART THE ORB WILL LOOSE!**

The Orb of Tarshi was as old as creation and had never felt power in such overwhelming quantities before and it could not absorb it as fast as it came to it, it was drowning in the flood of unstoppable force. Cracks began to form and the beam began to waver and fluctuate from the orb. It was now sinking toward the ground as groans came from the death ball.

I will not let you beat me said the orb, I have most of your powers in me now your getting weak.

NO.... NO YOU DON"T, NOW FACE OBLIVION STEALER OF SOUL!!

224

SHANE

The orb was crackling with energy when Destiny seized the orb in his grip and crushed it with a blast that would shatter a world.

Thousands of souls were instantly released and most of them materialized on the ground below me. They were looking at my lifeless body laying on the ground in a green haze. The energy being I was now picked up my own body and held it, looking it over because it isn't everyday you get to look at your own body from the outside. I then began to replace my life-force into the little body, which contorted as if it were being cooked.

At last all my soul was back inside of my shell and I still glowed like an pulsar. I stiffened and fell to the ground without moving.

Havax who was invisible ran up to me and said, don't touch him or you be vaporized. She slowly faded back into the visible plain and all the people or creatures bowed as she stepped up to me. She leaned down and a boy grabbed her hand and said you can't Shama or you'll be killed.

Havax said, thank you for your concern but it is his energies that run through my veins so I will be fine. Her tiny hand touched my face and all at once she knew that I had absorbed the Orb of Tarshi and she began to burn like the sun with energy.

She said I know what must be done, turned and said cover you eyes or you'll be blinded to the crowds.

SHANE

Havax began to look deep into her own heart then she opened her eyes and power flowed free like steam from a hot pot.

YOU WHO WERE CONCEIVED IN EVIL WILL NOW SERVE A HIGH PURPOSE, she began to cast.

The ground shook and the sky turned red as fire, lightning blasted great craters into the ground all around us and still she cast forth the bewitching tirade of magik. At this point all the energy turned green as in life or creation and that was her hearts desire, a world that was teaming life. Havax's body fell onto mine in utter exhaustion, she slept being totally spent.

Zer who was on his knees said, behold the wonder that is our world. Strangely, even Zer who had been atomized was granted a corporal body again once the Orb was destroyed.

All the crowds started to look up and around at the land and sky. Havax used all the energy from the orb to instill life to the lifeless land where she had lived her whole life. I came to and I could see Truth and Justice looking at me. I waved my hand and they smiled. A fight broke out behind me, a very large muscular scaly lizard man had Zer down and was fixing to disembowel him.

I placed my hand on the lizard man's shoulder and asked, are going to kill this man friend?

I sure am buddy he hissed in pleasure.

Why, I asked?

226

SHANE

Well, cause he is evil and he helped the orb imprison our souls, so he should die don't you think Lord Destiny?

I think there is a new world here to be enjoyed and lived in for you and your friend, I assured him. He let Zer go.

Zer said this is what I wanted when I found the globe, not to destroy as he looked around. The others did much the same now that their desert was a paradise that even Heaven could admire.

WE all set down and ate and drank and were generally enjoying the new prosperity of the land. Havax was asked to rule the world that her love had created and she agreed. In her first decree as ruler she made Zer her governor in acting for the peoples welfare. Zer bowed to Havax and excepted by cutting his hand and letting his blood run into the ground.

Then he said, I swear in blood that I will serve with all my life as the peoples protector.

Havax stood and asked if any person is opposed speak your mind.

The large man lizard stood and said, Shama I ask to be heard, then he bowed?

Havax said, we all await your thoughts lizard man.

SHANE

Thank you, I don't believe that I trust Zer, he has been evil before and although Sean who is Destiny has told us that Zer was cleans of evil I think a body of law protectors should be activated to make sure the peace is withheld and that no one will harm another again, he finish with a hard look for Zer.

Zer stood and bowed, may I speak Shama?

I give you the floor Governor, she said.

I think that, excuse me I don't know your name sir, Zer said to the lizard?

I am called Lizar, he said.

I then say we should ask lord Lizar to be our governor in charge of the peacemakers, demanded Zer.

The people were happy with Lizar's promotion to chief of peace. I sat not interfering with the politics of this new young world so full of hope but I saw someone very important being rudely overlooked and I knew that it was hurting his feelings, but he would not say anything.

Havax may I say something babe, I asked?

The look on her face was total surprise when she faced me, and all the people bowed low in my direction.

In our haste we forgot to give you the honor you deserve, I am

SHANE

sorry she said.

   Nonsense, I am your friend and asked no more than respect
as that, yet I am concerned that the truly great men are going
un-thanked and that I will not allow, I barked in anger. Father
come forth, stand with me and leader you as well.

   They came to rest on their knees in front of me, which I
thought was a great honor I didn't want but since they were
there I would use it. I raised my hand and there was total quiet.

   This man, father as I have called him because I know
no other, is able to see into a mans heart and the future and
has made my life richer from knowing his bravery and wisdom,
I explain to the huge crowd. I give him one more ability, the
gift of moving objects with his mind. I touched his head and
my hand was glowing bright yellow and so was the man. I say
rise master Seer and serve Havax well. He stood and opened his
eyes which were to remain bright yellow.

Seer said thank you Sean.

 I now call your attention to the leader as I know him, who
bravery and wisdom, sacrifice for his people has warmed my
heart. I give him the gift of indestructibility to be passed to a
suitable person of his chose before his death as are the Seer's
powers, I said. Stand master steel and serve Havax as her
advisor with Seer, you are the best and she will have need of you
both sooner that not, I told them.

SHANE

Havax was pleased at the chose I had made and so was the mob of people.

Later that week I was sitting on a tree branch near the river when Seer came up to me and said, one doesn't need to see the into the magik realm to tell that your troubled Sean.

I am your friend as well as your loyal follower, you can tell me what's on you heart.

You are not my follower but Havax's and I know your my friend, it is that I know soon I will have to leave again to face yet death and toil anew, I explained.

Seer said, I shall miss you and Havax doubly so Sean.

I know, I answered.

SHANE

SHANE

CHAPTER NINE: THE SEARCH FOR THE KEY

I left the new world that my love had created with my power in her, and although my power is surely grand it has not brought me any solstice in my life. I must find the master key and mend the time rip and rebalance the scale of power in the universe, if I am every going to get home once more. I stopped and closed my eyes and I focused on Nicky. The table in front of her started to glow and she, Jeanie, Justin and Bob stayed away from it then writing appeared in the middle, it said:

(Nicky, I am lost in a thousand   life times and a)
(googolplex of realities and worlds but I will)
(never forget your touch and your love as the lives)
(good bye, I WILL ALWAYS LOVE YOU...)
(YOUR LOVE Sean)
(LORD DESTINY!!!)

There it was plain as day when the table stopped glowing red hot from the heat because the table was solid rock, the message I had sent her in my mind. Nicky rushed her table and started to read, then cried hard. He still remembers me after all this time and see he loves me with all his heart was all she could think of.

Truth sat everyone down and said let me spin my tale for you as Justice has. I will start when Goth touched me and I p136 vanished. I fell into time and space just as my fellow keys

232

SHANE

had only unlike them I knew how to use my abilities right away.
I landed on a cloud where there was a little person in a big
robe, so I walked over and sat down. It raised it's head and
I was startled. I was looking at a face that look like the alien
from a movie, big teeth in two different mouths and small
glowing green eyes.

   Don't fear me because I am hideous by your standards,
rather except me because I am alien to you young Lord Truth, he
said.

   The moment was the most uncomfortable I have ever lived,
yet I was fascinated by the mind I felt searching my own.

   Are you here to teach me what I must learn on my journey, I
asked?

   No, I am here because you must know that there are forces at
work that are totally alien to you and your mind will be probing
them all, he said smiling I think.

 When the last word came forth my mind could feel every
thought, every feeling everything in creation even God, which
brought me to tears because of the pure beauty of life that I felt.
I had never felt so clean and alive before I touch or was touched
by the Holy Ghost, he told them.

The small ugly little alien said, excellent is it not my
boy.

233

SHANE

Yes, it is incredible, I said. However, when I looked at him he was not ugly anymore just different and in a way very beautiful I thought.

The alien said I feel the same way about you.

Who are you, I mean I can see all and know all but you don't seem to readable, I asked it.

I am from a race that are long dead because they worshipped war instead of God so they perished, yet I was given a reprieve if you will because I seen that it was God that was good and not war, it explained. I am Japo the Kim of the dead race of Kims and my planet is where we sit now.

I don't see a planet Japo, said I.

Well there isn't much left after all these millennia, cough Japo.

Millennia, how many has it been, I inquired?

Let me see, it has been a million two hundred thirty one I believe said Japo.

Wow your really old, huh, I offered?

I am as you would say older than dirt, he laughed.

Sitting on the cosmic cloud I saw suns being born, and

234

SHANE

worlds die but it all seem to be right with the scheme of thing,
until Vapor attacked Sean and as Destiny, Sean unleashed the
power in him that is alive and the universe wept for him, said
Bob to Jeanie and the other two. There is always a rift in
the balance of power when any of the keys cut loose, said Bob.

   Anyhow, Japo told me of events that had transpired in our
universe for thousands of years and that I needed to know them
all to be able to help Destiny in the fight to restore the
rightful balance. Further, he told me that I can't interfere
in any situation unless I am summoned and then I can only
advise.

   I have traveled around and seen things you can even image like
alien as small as your finger and titans as big as a battleship
and of course angels. Yet, my travels are not hard and lonely
such as Sean must endure, the rest you know from Justin, Bob
told them.

   The great hall was colder than I remembered when I reached
it for fifth time and darker still than it priorly was. The
key filled my thoughts, was the master key a man like me or
simply an object? Where do I look now? Why does the master
key bind the four brother keys as one, how does it work? WHY
ME, I thought to myself. Truth come and council me, I have need
of your knowledge brother. Truth bid his friend good day and
joined Sean it the hall of portals.

   What is it you want to ask me Ol'buddy, He inquired?

235

SHANE

I wish to know where the master key is and where is Hope at and why do I have to fight so hard and get no reward, I asked?

I will start backwards on your questions, first, the great ones must always make the ultimate sacrifice. Second, About Hope, I don't know that Hope has been chosen yet. Last, the master key is there Truth said as he pointed at A portal way behind me.   It has always been there Sean, he said to me with a smile.

Why the hell didn't you say that before Bob, I demanded!

You didn't ask and you know by now I can't interject unless you call for me to, he boldly explained.

The portal was very bright around the edge not like the others at all and it was spilling over with power that I could feel. I was about to enter and Bob said no! You may not enter without Justice and me by your side, because this is for the game Sean and you cannot loose or we all loose, Everything, our lives, the lives of every creature in all realities, Nicky's life... Do you see the weight you now carry, Truth growled at me sternly.

I nodded my head and said Justice I need you come to my aide. Justice kissed Jeanie goodbye as if he would not be coming back and she knew it. Reunited again the three Key of the universe entered the portal maybe never to return.

The moment was very solemn in the galley where Jeanie and Nicky were struggling not to start crying because it they did they

SHANE

may never stop again.

 Jeanie I can't be sad anymore or I'll die from loneliness, Nicky said with hot tears run down her smooth cheeks. Jeanie said, Justin said they were in no danger if they were together but he kissed me farewell, not until we meet again.

 In side the portal we were transported to a palace of impossible wealth and luxury where I sensed great power.

 Truth there is wild danger here and forces as strong as my own so be on guard for anything, even the furnishings may not be what seem, I said.

 Yes, they are what they seem Sean said a man with a weathered face standing in a doorway just beyond the next room.

 WE walked up to the doorway where our host was waiting for our approach. My hands were energized behind my back ready to blast anything to atoms if it turned hostile and so were Justice's.

 You need not ready for battle, you are welcome guests here, said the rugged looking man.

 Truth said he has it on him Sean. Does he have it or is he it, I asked without turning my burning gaze?

 I cannot absorb the energies of the key as your keys have absorbed you, said our host.

SHANE

The room around us was delightful to the sight, yet I was apprehensive even though I could sense no evil in our host.

Truth what do you know of this man, I required?

I know that he has the master key and that he is very old, yet his soul is fresh to the senses, Truth offered. Justice what do you thing son, I ask?

I think I'll reserve judgment at the moment and wait to see how things unravel dad, was his answer.

I know you from the little town in the woods when I lost fifteen years off my life, don't I, I said.

Yes, it was me who told you how to get back home, then made it possible for you to escape the trap that was set for you by Goth, he spit after he said his name. Goth?

After a short walk into a room filled with pillows and soft chairs we sat ready to hear our host weave his tale. It started a long time ago when Goth was young and still living he was made keeper of the sacred stones which could be used to created or destroy. Well he was a good man then but one day after years of perfect service he was called by the council of elders that guide the universe, he continued. Goth obeyed their summons and came before them. They told him he was to be replace as keeper of the sacred stones, but what they didn't tell him was it was because they wanted him to join the council and be an elder, he went on. Goth was crushed at the thought of guarding the

238

stones all of those years and never once attempting to use them, now replaced, it was more than he could bear.

Further, before they could tell him the good news he pulled two of the six stones from his pocket and said if I can't have these stones than no one else will either and he used the stones power to kill the council.

However, he didn't get the job done because I and one other were not there and survived. I am council Fect, he concluded.

The tale was a good one and we were a little confused at this development. Frankly I liked this guy for some reason I wanted to believe him but I felt since he had the Master Key to bind the other three and one unknown to us, he had to power to deceive us.

Truth is he telling the truth, or is he lying to us, I asked?

I heard no untruth come from his lips, then again he has the master key doesn't he, said Bob.

Would you like to examine the key boys, asked Fect?

Justin said, heck ya, are going to give it me peacefully or do we have to fight for it?

If I give it to you what will you do with it, Fect asked in a serious tone?

239

SHANE

WE all looked at each other and then at Fect for a brief moment, then with a sigh I broke the silence.

Wait he's right we can give it back to Goth just incase he is nuts, I exclaimed in disappointment.

May I see the key asked Bob.

The key was not unlike the ones we were given at the start of our quests only it had a spot on each face for our keys to attach to it. I took out my key and began to put it into place when Fect tackled me and yanked the key from my hand.

Are you so ready to die Sean, if you place your key on here without the other three at the same moment you will be absorbed, yelled Fect.

I didn't know, I said.

It is okay but I think the key is best kept in my hands for now, at least until Hope is chosen, said Fect.

Can you tell me anything about Hope, Truth asked him?

Hope is that which is always renewed in all mankind every time you need it and when things are their darkest Hope is a shining light said Fect.

Tell me how Goth got our keys and why didn't he use them to get the master key from you, Bob asked?

SHANE

Well, as I told you Goth used two stones to kill the council, those stones are now this and he held up the master key as a visual aide. The other stones were turned into key of the universe because they house the powers of the council in them, Fect explained. Justice was about to speak and Fect held up a hand and wave to him to let him continue.

Further, Goth could not use the keys because the souls within would not allow it, and the master key can't be absorbed because it is two stones in one, Fect added. Moreover, Goth realized that he did not get all of the council so he hunted us and in the ensuing battles he lost his life so to speak, therefore couldn't wield the power of any of the keys anymore so I took the Master key because it plus all the other key combine gives ultimate power and he could bring himself back from the dead, he finished.

And Goth went to find us who were going to succeed where he could not, great said Justice.

In the hours that passed Fect told us of the plan he had worked on for a thousand years to rid the universe of Goth and his evil followers such as Vapor who Destiny buried. The part of the plan that Fect had not counted on way the absence of Hope and the cleverness of Goth in almost tricking us into giving him back full power and his life.

I told my friends that I must rest on it for a while, so I adjourned to a bed in another room to sleep.

241

SHANE

Meanwhile Fect told the other keys that I would have to be the one who sacrifices himself to the power key in order to complete the cycle and restore the balance.

I am not quite sure from where I heard the voice or if I really heard it, but it said take heart brother, Hope is born and your no longer without it, The it was gone and I opened my eyes and I did feel better even if was just my imagination.

Justice I just had a dream that Hope was with us now, I told him.

I felt a trimmer in the power balance too, he said.

Truth can you locate Hope now, I asked?

No, Hope is still shielded from even my endless sight but I know someone who might be able to help, Truth said.

Japo the Kim join us, Bob raised his hands and started to cast his energies out in search of the ugly little alien friend and mentor he knew.

The room filled with light when Japo the Kim faded into view in the middle of the room.

Greetings young Key masters, and one old one I see, he said.

SHANE

This is truly a surprise I have not seen you since before the death of the council old comrade, said Fect.

That's what I thought, I could not read Japo and I know that it takes a being of great power to block my mind, he is the other surviving council member, Truth said with conviction.

Can you help us locate Hope Japo and guide us to the right place to finish off Goth, Fect asked?

The ugly four jawed mini alien walked to a room that was mostly empty and then turned for a moment and said only Truth may stay because where we go now is not for you others.

What, now you wait just a damned minute, I have to bare the burden of saving reality and I can't see where your going, Bull Shit pal, I growled.

Justin started to grab me to help calm me but I started glowing orange and Justin changed his mind and stepped away.

Japo said, my friend it is because of the great weight your shoulders alone that I wish to spare you anymore heartache, there are event that are to come that will hurt you more than any magik ever could and you won't be able to stop them. So you decide son what is right.

I guess your right I'll stand off so you can do what you must, I answered.

243

SHANE

Minutes turned to hours, and hour to days, days to weeks and still they cast without rest until they found what they needed to finish. One day while Fect, Justin and I were playing a hologram fighting game Truth emerged and made a beeline for us but he collapsed four feet away from pure and utter exhaustion.

I said, Justin go for Japo, I will get lover boy to his bed, and that's just what I did.

Japo as it turned out was not as bushed as Bob and recovered in a few days where Bob took a week to rejuvenate.

Out with it what did you find guys, I asked them anxiously?

I found Goth but I had to wear down his metal defenses before I could probe his mind, but he won't be causing us any trouble for a while because I scrambled his eggs if you know what I mean, said Truth.

We all laughed at the mental image he just painted for us of Goths brain being scrambled.

What is he up to Bob, Justin inquired?

He doesn't know we are on to him, and he still plans to recreate himself after he kills us, he is in a neutral plan where his power is all and we have no hope of reaching him there, Truth explained.

What about you Japo, what did you find out about Hope, asked

SHANE

Justin?

**Hope is a long journey from here and needs us to break free
from it's shell, he said.**

SHANE

SHANE

CHAPTER TEN: THE SEARCH FOR HOPE.

   The journey that Japo spoke of was not going to be through a portal but a space voyage though the universe that would take a normal man six hundred years if he could live that long, but we ... ARE NOT normal are we.

   Fect said let me show you boys something, and he turned through a door that led to a party of his home that we had never known was there. Before us was a spacecraft of a superior design far advanced as a caveman to one of us, yet we seemed to know of it's workings through the previous Key masters memories.

   This is the last of it kind, an artifact of a one great race that was destroyed by the greed of Goth and his minions, said Fect.

It is yours and it is as living as you and me so remember it at time has a mind of it's own, do not forget this, said Fect.

   The supplies were loaded as were the extra stuff like the hologram game for recreation while we were ripping through space. There were no long farewells, just until we meet in the final conflict and we entered the ship to leave and the door to the ship would not close even though Justin was reefing on it.

   Ship would you button us up so we may depart please, I

SHANE

asked?

I recognize Destiny and I obey. The hatch slammed shut and the ship said, to your seat please, I move fast when I take off so buckle up.

WE made our way into the cockpit off this fabulous ship that would carry us the Gods playground. WE buttoned down and I said, okay StarRider hit it. Boy did he ever hit gas, we were miles away in seconds.

StarRider was very alive and he was incredibly knowledgeable about history and star charting, he even bragged that Fect and him had seen the four corners of the universe and that the universe was ever growing bigger.

Where are we headed Star, I inquired?

We are headed to that dot there and a pointer appeared on the scene near the dot of light he had indicated.

How long do you think it will take us to get there ship, said Truth?

Twenty years or so but your an eternal and don't age so what's the difference?

I like this ship, I said.

The ship said, I like you too, your very strong so the pirates

SHANE

won't be any trouble for you, boss.

Pirates are you joking or what I blurted?

No, I am afraid that they are as real as you, haven't your travels taught you that you just about anything is possible if you don't confine your examples to human standards?

Point well taken ship, I said.

Can you detect other spacecraft before they are upon us, asked Justin?

My technical equipment is far advance compared to any other that we may encounter on our journey, stated the ship proudly.

That sounds great but what about weapons ship and shields from there weapons, asked Justin?

You ask allot of questions Justice, I can repel almost anything form of assault, explained StarRider.

For weeks the trip was totally uneventful and we took in the sights in space since none of us ever dreamed that someday we would be roaming the far reaches of the unknown cosmos. However, as we discovered it was not unknown at all.

The first sign of an alien civilization that I noticed was a small outpost on a massive planetoid.

249

SHANE

Hey ship is that a space port down there, I eagerly inquired?

Affirmative, boss, was my answer.

What do you guys think about stopping and stretching our legs, I asked?

Why not dad, said Justin.

Yeah, I think it might be a hoot to check out a space port, Bob said.

The ship took the appropriate steps toward a landing on the pad with strange ruins on it. They are a blessing to all the stop here, said Truth.

After we touched down, we all got ready to depart when the ship said," beware of this place because Goth knows you search for Hope and will come this way".

Thanks ship, we'll keep our eye to the ground, I told him.

Very good, said the ship and the hatch popped open.

Despite the technical advances it looked like a airport, yet it was something new to see. I felt like a little boy in an amusement park and from the look on the faces of my companions they felt the same way. If we were going to find Hope we might as well get some help here or make some friends right now or hire a guide I thought to myself. This is really a

250

SHANE

spaceport like in the movies, I always wanted to go into space but I never dreamed it would happen and now that has I have ever intention of enjoying it. The ship touched down.

   A man in a hood approached us from across the far end of the landing pad.

Bob said, don't worry his thoughts are of greetings not assassinations.

   Do we look worried, Bob, Justin asked?

   Let me put it this way, if you guys down get some R/R soon , you'll probably explode, Jested Bob.

The man stood a full two heads above us when he stopped in front of us. He tossed back the hood and said welcome to our little port, your honored guests here, feel free to wonder around or ask for someone to guide you, it is your choice.   He was very tall, at least eight feet and he was a Cyclops which even though I had seen many things in my world hopping journeys was still very interesting to me.

   I am Sean and this is my son Justin, he's our friend Bob, I manage to spout. Who are you sir, I asked?

I am called Prylor Lasget, he offered in good faith.

Prylor is a governor in his social system Bob said to us.

SHANE

That is correct Prylor is my title, Lasget said to Bob. He turned and led us off the port and into the base itself which was cut deep into the planetoid.

The were thousands of people or creatures there but at this point they was no difference to me. This station was a veritable smorgasbord of cultures and foods of every color and smell, all of which was better than the one before but all of them made me drool. Truth followed Lasget to the local library to learn the history of Lasgets people. Truth could have used his powers to read the knowledge of Lasget's people, from Lasget's mind but Bob felt like me about using his powers needlessly. Justin went to see what kind of games they had here on this planetoid. He found them quickly when some of the locals heard he was interested. There was the normal kind of computer games and then Justin found the game he was looking for, the big game that is their favorite. It was two men facing a table on opposite sides with controls on the terminals just in front of each player. he game itself was one warrior for each man that fought with magik and weapons until one warrior was dead. Here is the point of the game, when you loose your life-force is drawn into the other player, if you loose twice in a row you would die from the process. Justin stood there until he was sure he knew the game as well as any who were regular players.

Who is next to loose their energy to me, said a big alien.

I'll have a try if nobody objects, said Justin.

A little man said no don't he'll drain you.

252

SHANE

Justin only patted him on the back and said don't worry.

The big alien said, come sit here stranger.

Justin took his place and the game began and Justin's man was killed easily.

You loose said the big alien. He sucked off some power which Justin had an infinite supply.

  Play again boy, said his foe?

Yes, thank you Justin said.

  This time the game started and Justin's character was winning and at the moment that he was about to kill the other character, the big aliens creation won the game. Justin just smiled and the big alien said none can beat me boy and he drained even more energy this time but Justin still wanted to play. The game started a third time but this time Justin was aware that his opponent was cheating, so when he began to win Justin used his powers to override the circuits that would have made his foe win and this time he won.

  The big alien stood and said impossible!

  No, your little device that helped you cheat is no longer working, said Justin.

SHANE

The alien rushed Justin and hit him in the stomach but his massive hand only bounced off.

Justin turned his powers up until he was glowing, then he grabbed the alien and forced him to his knees.

I am Justice and you have stolen allot of these peoples energies from them, now you are going to give it all back.

The big alien started to glow and then energy flowed free of him and into the crowd until he was nearly drained, then at that point Justice broke it off.

Never play the games again or next time I won't stop to save your life.

Meanwhile, I had found a place that was very much like a nightclub from earth. The creature who was on the stage did not have arms, legs, or a mouth for that matter yet it was telling jokes about things I had no knowledge about and it was still funny. It noticed I was laughing so it came to my seat and said, look here I'm crackin this guy up and he doesn't know the hell I am talking about.

True, I am not familiar with the subject but your delivery is excellent, I said.

That's not what dominos said when they fired me, he cracked. Everybody laughed.

SHANE

Another alien noticed that I was a stranger there and he offered
me a drink of some pink liquid substance. I realized that it might
be poison to me, but I was curious as to the taste of this
booze. Why not, I accepted. He pored the liquid into two fountain
shaped glasses.

This is the best stuff in this galaxy friend, he said proudly.

I drank. At first the bar seemed to be full of strange creatures
when I entered it, but now it was just full. Whenever I drained
my glass it was filled with more of the sweet pink nectar. The
night came and went and everyone was a new friend in this place
so far from my home. I woke up to the sound of people walking
around in the hall outside of the room where I slept the night
before. How did I get here was my first thought and where is my
cloths? The door swung in and Justin's mug peeked around the
doorjamb at me.

How do you feel fish-boy, he said?

 Fish-boy what's that suppose to mean son?

You drank enough of that pink stuff to swim in dad, he told me.

Where is Bob at, I grunted as one eye closed? He is still in the
library studying the stars and their histories, Justin filled me in.

Okay let's fetch him and set sail boyo, I said.

   The ship had drawn a fair amount of visitors in our absence.

255

SHANE

It seen us coming and said, good morning master.

Are you ready to roll ship, I asked?

Ready and standing by for your orders, it said.

Good show ol'boy, I said. Plot a course for the system where we will find our brother Hope, I instructed the ship.

Course plotted and laid in Sean, the ship reported. Is everyone ready, asked the ship?

Yes, Said Bob.

Me too, answered Justin.

StarRider punch it, I ordered.

The ship took off at it's usual bat out of hell speed and we were on to the next adventure that might show it's head.

The journey was going to be exciting said the ship.

Good show, let's see what's out there that is still undiscovered and untouched or spoiled, I said.

In the third month since we left the space station the trip brought us passed a nova, a planet where life was just beginning and some friendly aliens that we stopped long enough to trade with.

SHANE

All of us were having a good time just playing galactic explorer
and we even started calling ourselves the Star Riders, which
please the ship no small amount that we chose his name to bare.
Our travels took us across the universe where we picked up
quite a rep for being heroes and I must admit that for the first
time I was enjoying the powers that were forced on me and I let
Nicky know what was happening on a regular basis by scribing
notes on a fresh piece of flat wood each day that Nicky
provided. Justin and Bob just popped out and then returned when
they were finished with their visits home which they knew was
hurting me since I could not go home until the quest was
finished.   On a day where we were going over Tactics for
boarding and retrieval with minimal detection, the ship
suddenly shifted, which through us against the bulkhead.

Ship what the hell just happened, asked Justin?

 I am experiencing an anomaly in my micro circuitry I am
embarrassed to say said the ship.

So your sick, like the computer flu Hugh, said Bob?

Yes, Said the ship.

 How bad is it ship, what's the damage bud, I asked?

 My defense grid is still up, but my propulsion is down as well as
life support and general ship on board internal systems, he said.

SHANE

That's just great, now we are stuck out here in the middle of nowhere, complained Justin.

It was many days of intense search for the systems that were affected by the computer flu. The ship was taking it badly, because he was very old and never needed repairs, which he pointed out on a regular basis.

I told the ship that everybody gets down time sooner or later and that why should he be any different.

This caused him to chill and actually enjoy being taken care of for a change. However, Bob and Justin were getting uptight as the delay went on longer than expected, I needled them as often as I could which always ended up in a squirt gun fight.

How alive are you really ship, Justin asked him?

I am as alive as you but in a different way of coarse, answered the living ship.

After a few weeks the ship began to get better but not enough to move on. Justin and Bob started to get worried that we were not going to be able to protect Hope when he is empowered. What should we do Sean, Bob asked?

Your the one with the infinite knowledge and see the past and future Bob, you tell me, I said to him. Ship if we provide you with enough extra energy could you heal yourself, Bob inquired?

SHANE

Yes, I believe that would do it sir, answered the ship, but it must be done from the outside of me. It was cold in space but we set to our task as if it were a warm sunny day in July. Since we didn't need a spacesuit to walk in space because we are immortal and don't require oxygen to live, we went outside the ship on all three corners. In place, I expressed the ommand to engage telepathically to my brother keys and we all started to glow bright green like three small suns.

Are you ready ship, Truth asked?

Affirmative, said the ship!

The energy from my right hand shot to Justice's left hand and his energies shot forth to Truth in the same manner and Truth's to me, until we had made a circle of energy that surrounded the ship entirely. The craft began to glow as well until it said, I have had enough energy to do the job master's.

Good show, well have a little extra for those emergencies that might pop up, I said.

The ship was totally rejuvenated in a few hours and we were on our way once more to find Hope. In the near future we would find that unleashing our energies to heal the ship, had a much wider effect than we realized. Since we had not seen or heard anything about Goth or his goon patrol we had back-bunkered him temporarily. We also forgot about the pirates since we had never seen them up close, but all of that was just about to change. In orbit of the sixth planet in a three star galaxy was

SHANE

the biggest ship I have ever seen.

Damn, would you take a look at that size of that baby, said Justin.

 It does not see us though said the ship.

 Why not ship, Justin wanted to know?

Because we are cloaked, it is one of the features of my defense grid master Justice, explained the ship.

 Ship scan their ship and report what type of defense grid they are sporting, said Truth.

Okay said the ship, the have a fifty plasma firing bank and a class eleven shield, plus ten thousand warhead projectiles.

 What class is your shield Justin asked?

 I am equipped with a shield if it was in a class system that would rate class three thousand and to answer your next question I have ten forward gun batteries, six side and ten rear, said the ship. Further, have two hundred shrapnel missiles on board, and each battery is a pulsar projector, in other words if they shoot at us I can absorb that energy amplify it and blow them to hell, the ship expanded.

 Well I can't say that you didn't tell us when we came aboard

SHANE

that you were the stuff, but I must say you are incredible ship, I said in amazement.

   The pirate ship didn't see us as we pulled right next to it in orbit. Onboard the pirate ship the first mate said captain we are getting a strange echo from our own ship's signature.

 It's nothing besides who would be dumb enough to attack us, our ship is a hundred times as big as any other in the universe, so stop worrying.

We sat in the shadow of the great pirate ship for several hours, because it was doing anything wrong but we knew it was only a matter of time. Finally, a ship twice as large as ours came through the system and the pirate ship began to power up it's weapons and thrusters. We just tagged along to make sure that it was not only business that they were doing, but as we guessed they were not going for a friendly visit.

The pirate ship launched a warhead aimed for the other ships engine section, said the ship.

Blast it ship and any other that come from the colossus I told him as I walked over and study the markings on the intended target. Raise that ship Justin on a secure channel and tell them that the Star Riders will protect them and to move behind the pirate ship, I ordered.

   Okay Dad, consider it done, Said Justin.

SHANE

 The pirate ship was in a state of confusion at their warhead being blown to atoms. The first mate was explaining his shadow theory to the captain again when a bright light engulfed their bridge. When the light faded they saw three figures standing together in the center of the room, who were dressed in the same uniforms, which said Star Riders on the right arms and their names on the other.

 I am Destiny and your a cowardly pirate who is to lazy to work for a living, so you kill lots of innocent hard working people to fatten your pockets, well no more I said as I walked up to the captain shaking my finger.

Behind me Justin and Bob were doing the shame on you hand gestures, which made me laugh. The pilot pulled on weapon and was going to shoot me ,but Justice raised his hand without turning his head to look at the man and vaporized him. The crew were horrified, Justin just smiled and pulled his hand back to his side.

   Now listen up pal your going to act as the protectors of the galaxy or the dust of it, the choice is yours but don't make me want to long or I'll choose and you won't like that I can guarantee, I told him with a stern look and flames coming from my fingertips.

   You don't have that kind of power and even if you did, you don't have the authority to make that decision, he said.

 Fair enough, I shall show you the level of force that I could

SHANE

apply to you, I said as I turned and walked right out of their ship
into space. Do you see that asteroid over there, I am going to
turn it into a sun because this system needs another, I said as I
turned to them.

I let my energies flow until I was glowing as bright as a sun,
then I pointed my hands at the rock and it sprang to life, a
new sun born. I walked back into the pirate ship and said
CHOOSE OR DIE!!!

 The captain said we would rather die than let you dictate our
life for us, he said as the First mate shot him in the back. The
captain turned, looked his crew in the face and fell dead.

 I am captain now and I say it is better to keep the piece than be
in pieces, said the first mate.

The crew was with him and reach an answer by vote which was
unanimous.

 I have raise the solar governors and explained to them what
you asked of them, they agreed that the pirate ship is the best
equipped to be the peacekeepers of the space way.

Further, they will grant you supplies aplenty when you need
them, the ship told me and the new pirate captain.

I offer you this gift I said to the captain as I put my hand on
his head, and he began to glow. My hand began to glow so bright
that you could not look at it without getting welding type

SHANE

flash burns on your eyes. The captain shook as if he would come apart at the seams but did not, all at once he let out a blood curdling scream and fell to the floor in a quivering heap of smoking flesh.

When he opened his eyes he said I am un-harm able and have incredible powers, why?

I gave you them Because your crew might decide to shoot you in the back and there are some mean sons-a-bitches out there that you'll be expected to bring to justice and they have powers to, that's why, I told him. Go in peace and good luck.

We transported ourselves back to the ship and rejoined the quest for Hope. Once under way the ship told us that our journey was not much longer, because it had found a hole in space that would save years of traveling time if we dare brave it. Of course, we were going to brave it, there was never a doubt in the ships mind as to that.

I think we should give this hole in space a try if it will bring us to Hope quicker, I said as I took the center seat on the bridge. The others didn't say anything but I knew that was because I really had the final say in all matters, so they knew I only asked to be nice. I thought of how Hope would look and act and if we would know him when we saw him, I didn't know. The hole laid ahead and to the right of our planned course. I thought what if this is not a good idea and we get hopelessly lost in some alien galaxy where we aren't more powerful than our foes and what about Goth, could this be some elaborate trap for me and the

SHANE

boys. However, without any hesitation I ordered the ship into the hole. The instant the ship moved even a little inside the hole it was sucked all the way in and was thrust at a incredible speed in some unknown direction because it was black as midnight and we had no sensor feed from the ship, because he was dizzy from the inertia. The entire trip took only minutes and we were clear of the hole, in the starlight again suddenly. The ship took chart readings and reported that we had traveled two million three hundred thousand light years in five minutes, at his best guess and we were not alone at the moment.

Shields up, defense grid on, let's not be caught with our pants down shall we, I said with a little humor. Scan them ship and report all significant information that might be useful, I stated in a hurry just realizing that they are probably doing that right now.

The ship reported that they had no arms at all and they asked for our help because they are lost. Further, they had no fuel to speak of and are stranded.

Are they humanoid, alien, asked Justin

Yes, and they are all female, said Bob with a twisted little smile. They appear to be powerful telepaths from a planet of women that is in badly need of some new D.N.A. for a recharge, he added.

We allowed their ship to dock with StarRider so that we could provide the help that they needed, little did we know that the

265

SHANE

only help that they wanted was some steamy coupling for refertilization of their race. When the airlock was opened the first one of them walked through and stopped looking a little afraid, but smiling none the less. She was followed by five more women all in a long hooded cloak of emerald. The first girl stepped sideway and a red manned women stepped forth. She pulled back the hood and let the cloak fall nearly off her shoulders but it was held up by full firm breasts that the instant focal point of the conversation.

Greetings, we are the women of Lon, and I am captain Mira, they are my crew and we are at your disposal sir, she concluded. Must we stand in the airlock or can we enter, asked another of the hauntingly beautiful Witch-women of Lon.

Come in and be welcome, you are our guests until we find a way to help you, then you can be on your way, I said.

There is no hurry, we like to be picked up by three good looking men and helped as often as we can, said Mira with a penetrating look at me. You see we travel around looking for suitable men to donate genetic materials for our continued existence she added with an gesture at me. She led the six of them to our galley, where they all waited for the three of us to join them.

Mira said all we have to thank you with is ourselves. She gestured and all the women dropped their cloaks. The sight of six nearly genetically perfect nude women set my soul on fire. They told us that they wanted to mate with us to help expand their

SHANE

gene pool. Bob was more than happy to assist in a noble, worthy cause he told them.

Mira told me that each of them wanted to sleep with each of us to great increase the genetic recombination. However, they must wait until she was done with me first. I didn't mind because although each of them were strikingly beautiful and sexual, I liked Mira the most. There are six of us and three of you so at any time two of us will make love to each of you men, Mira explained. Tess and Bess the twins will go with Bob and Nina and Fir shall take care of all of Justin's loving this time, Mira said. Little Runa and I shall pleasure our host , she added. Runa was the youngest and she was a red head like Mira, yet her body was as nearly developed as her senior partner and she was afraid I could see the difference. Mira laid on my bed on her back and beckoned me over to her but my interest was on Runa at the moment. She is on her first mission and has never been with a man, you see we all practice our lovemaking skills on each other or dream lovers in a meditative state until we are chosen to search space, Mira told me. She likes you very much but is afraid, although she had the highest sexual arousal scores of any girl ever chosen to our genetic pirate fleet, she added.

Are you really the best lover there is in all your people Runa, I hungrily inquired?

Yes, I seem to have natural talent for lovemaking, but only with androids and Mira lately, said Runa as she looked into my eyes for the first time. I want to feel you against of me but I'm afraid I

267

SHANE

won't be able to satisfy you and you will scorn me, she said shyly.

Androids huh, how does that work? Are they life like, you know like a man or are they different, I asked her seriously?

   I walked over to her and put my arms around her naked body squeezing her bottom. Since she wasn't facing me I turned her toward me and I kissed her as gentle as I knew how, fondling her perfect breasts and fingering her nipples which were totally erect at this point. I was more than a little excited at the moment so I guided Runa to my bed where I laid her on her back. I kissed her from her mouth to her toes making long stops at her breasts and other regions, which brought the woman in her. And when my tongue was teasing her earlobe, she finally relaxed. Then Mira undressed me and the three of us cuddled for days, until we got hungry and stopped. To my surprise the galley had everyone aboard in it eating when we arrived.

Hey dad what's up, Justin said with a wink as Nina bit his neck.

I don't think that any of us should switch partners, said Mira even though it would help our planet. All of the Lon women were happy to hear that because they all fell in love with their man and didn't want to switch.

   I think that you ladies need to know our secret if we are going to stay together, I announced.

I already know said Runa as she pressed her lovely body harder

SHANE

against my chest, your the Star Riders, heroes!

 Yes, that is true but we are way more than that love, I said.

They all look at me as I explained the journeys that we Had
taken and the quest for Hope, which we must find so we could go
home again. At the point I showed them who we really were and
the burden of that which we all had to carry.

 Mira was the first to smile at the prospect of having a baby boy
for her first child. Having a baby with a eternal or immortal
appealed to her very much and she said so many times.

You see in their service they go into space find a man and get
pregnant with his child but they always had girls and this time
they would have boys if we helped. Runa never let her grip on
me loosen through the whole story, as I noticed the other
women also had never let go of Bob or Justin.

 This is a great moment for us to be your mates, because we will
be the mothers of eternals, men who will have sons or daughters,
but not only girls, Mira expressed with great joy, then seemed
sad for all of a sudden.

Your going to have to leave us aren't you, asked Tess to Bob,
who was holding Bess and Tess close to himself?

 No, not really, you see we live a very long time and since we
love you we will always come back, said Bob. I have nowhere to
go after this quest so I will be coming to live with you girls when

SHANE

it over to raise my kids. By the way how long do you live and
how many kids will you have, Bob asked.

 We live to between two and three hundred years but only our
brains age not our bodies so what you see is what you get as
long as we live, answered Bess with a smile then a kiss for
Bob.

 We closed the air lock and towed their ship to their planet
behind us. Meanwhile each of us was loving the new found loves
in our life who as it seemed would be in our life for along time
which made me happy. When we approached their planet of Lon
a fleet of ships approached fast from the planet. The lead ship
hailed us.

What have you done with Mira and her crew the voice said? Then
the ships surrounded our ship and lock on weapons.

This is Captain Mira and they have brought us home Sisters so
let them pass in peace and be happy for us all, I will explain on
the planet, she replied.

We landed on the planet near a city of flowers and art, where all
the people were beautiful naked women. The hatch opened and
all nine of us exited Star Rider and walked down the gangplank
to the crowd below. All of the women were touching us when we
walked into the crowd and apparently they all wanted to mate
with us but Runa spoke up.

Get back these are our men and if any of you want to be with

270

SHANE

them you'd better behave yourself, said Runa.

This man is mine and Mira's, If he chooses maybe yours but first, last and always he is mine said Runa harshly!

Well said added Tess, I have no intention of letting anyone put their hands on Bob except Bess and if Bob chooses maybe one of you!

A women with a cape of gold came through the crowd and said, we sent you out into space to find D.N.A and you did, but you also brought back three beautiful men and all of us are love starved, so you must allow us to mate with then or we shall die of loneliness, she said as she walked up to me and put her hand on my chest.

She was very beautiful and was obviously the leader of her people. Her body was as all of the women of Lon were, perfect.

There is another way I said to the women as I felt her breasts, we could bring other good men here for you, but I agree, if Mira and Runa don't object to your being with us. They shook their heads in approval when I looked at them. The leader women liked my idea about bring more men because there were millions of women on Lon and no men or diseases. It was basically paradise.

Justin , Bob and I gathered in the middle of a large empty field and cast forth our energies to some old friends. A ship suddenly appeared in the sky over the city and it was big.

271

SHANE

The captain of the ship was standing beside me a few moments later.

Hello pirate Durn, I said. I have brought you and your crew here because these lovely ladies have no men and you have thousands of men. He looked at all the naked women.

I said, yes your are supposed to sleep with them that is why your here. He just smiled as ten girl took him into a building. The rest of the crew came and went, found women who swore to them and only them aplenty, then did their duties on a daily basis. They also work their jobs on the ship. Justin and Bob went with their lovely mates and I didn't see them for a while. I settled in the quarts they gave me and looked around to see what this planet had other than beauties. However, babes was it's chief export and I had to spend time with mine. The leader's name was Sira who was the most intelligent women I ever made love with, she didn't talk in bed much though. Still, my favorite lover was still Runa, who's passion was as limitless as the sky, I loved her more than I knew. Mira was the best athlete on Lon and her body was a sign of it, and although I did love her, it wasn't like Runa and Nicky I thought to myself on a daily basis. A year later I was still on Lon and I had three new little brothers for Justin to play with, but he was to busy with my grandkids to notice his siblings.

Bob also had new baby sons to show he had dropped in on Lon. It had been a good year and the women were so in love with us and thankful that I had brought the pirates here as well.

272

SHANE

However, I knew we would have to go rejoin the quest for Hope and home which this place now qualified as. I made daily ventures to the ship so he didn't feel that we had abandoned him for the obvious pleasures on the planet.

 Today as I spoke to the ship it said we are here, "Hope is below on Lon master". I guess the look on my face was pretty astonished, because the ship said, "I believe that you know Hope and have for a year".

  I thought for a moment that he must be one of the pirates but as it turned out later I would find that was not the case.

 I told the ship that I was not happy at him keeping this information from me all this time.

The ship explained that Hope came to him and asked that this year be give to all four of the Keys to get to know each other because the coming battle with Goth was to be for all of our lives and could wait until the children were born.

I left for the planet to find Hope and to get Justin and Bob ready to go after Goth. In the city were all of my friends and loved ones together waiting for me when I arrived. Okay, I thought who is Hope, which one and why not show himself it is time? Just then I saw something that made my mouth drop open, around the neck of one of the people nearest to my heart hung the Key of Hope in plain view. There would be no choice, only an explanation of why Hope never reveal who they were to me. It was Runa my

SHANE

favorite love, I know that there was something special about her but this was big.

 I am sorry, I couldn't tell you before my baby was born, he has two eternals for parents, so this planet has received it's Hope for the future, she said almost in tears.

 How did you conceal it from me, we're lovers, I asked?

 I have the same abilities that each of you do except I am Hope the light of something better, Your Never Without Hope, was her answer.

I walked over and put my arms around her, kissed her as I had every night for a year and said, okay let's go finish this crap with Goth and go get Nicky, come home, live happily ever after.

SHANE

SHANE

CHAPTER ELEVEN: THE QUESTS END.

When we were on the ship to leave Hope said we don't have to travel back the way you came, why don't we transport back to save time. I explained to the ship that we were going to transport him and ourselves through a time shift in the plains of reality. He wasn't exactly thrilled at the prospect of a jump shift that was so big, but he was also interested in the experience so we all joined hands and we jump shifted the next moment. One of us could have preformed the shift solo but Joining hands was a show of solidarity. We emerged next to the home of Fect, who was joined by Japo. They waved to us as the might StarRider pulled up to the curb. The ship seemed sad and regretted the loss of the mighty crew of eternals that he had shared so many adventures with.

Good-by, my master there will be no more like you to pilot me across the far reaches of space.

Actually ship there is a new crop of young Star Riders being raised, my children and the kids of the other eternals so you will have another mighty crew, I for one am not ready to give you up yet though old friend, I said as I turned to leave the ship.

Then I am standing by when ever you need me, my master!

Fect was very pleased to see us all in one piece back for the

SHANE

final play of this deadly game we play.

You are to be congratulate I hear, three little baby boys and so
does Bob and Justin, well done, little eternals will do the cosmos
some good. He dispensed with the niceties and got to the
important topics, such as the whereabouts of our old friend Goth
and his followers. Goth is in one of the netherworlds, in a plain of
reality that he is nigh all powerful, in this place he can be
very dangerous and he must be defeated by your will alone.
Once he is defeated you must attach all four of your keys to the
master key, this will give the chosen one the ability to send Goth
to his final reward.

That is just fine but if we place all our key on the master, won't
that leave the other three helpless to attack, I asked Fect with a
sharp tone in my voice to let him know I was not happy at this
plan?

No, you are the four key of the universe and you will be until
you are replaced by new key holders, until that time nothing
other than God has more power than you, he answered.
However, know this, the one who holds all the keys at once will
become a homo supreme, which is the step above homo
superior that you now are, he added very sternly, that person is
going to be one with the universe and is absolute law in it.

WE all put our heads together and our hearts to find it in
ourselves to do whatever was going to be required in this, the
final conflict. We did not however talk of who would bare the
burden of the supreme sacrifice because it was a given that it

277

SHANE

was my cross to bare and was not open for debate. I thought of
when I was little and fished with my great grand pappy Macky on
the banks of all the rivers and creeks in Idaho, it seemed that
life was about catching or being caught, in this case that
philosophy applied. I think that Truth and Hope were reading my
mind and they saw my meaning in the fishing memories from my
childhood. They also knew that I felt responsible for their lives.
They left me to my solitude once more as they had to so many
time in the past.

I was going to face not Goth but my own self for what I was, not
a hero or a god but just a man who needed closure in his life.
Unfortunately for me it would come via a fight for the known
universe. To play or not to play this deadly game we had to play.
"shit what a bummer ". Then again I thought " You are to be
congratulated, for the ground you have already taken".

Japo and Bob went into there temple of sorts and began
to cast forth their incredible mental powers to ferret out the
scumbag Goth who drug us into this mess in the fist place.

   Meanwhile I was making a note for Nicky when Runa came in
and sat next to me on the bed where I was at. She was definitely
reading my mind being a natural born telepath and now receiving
the powers of the Key of Hope, she could not resist and I knew
that. Further, she loved me with all her heart and would see my
thoughts without disturbing them, but I could feel her in my mind
and she knew it, so I thought warm thoughts of her and a good
future that made her smile.

278

SHANE

Reading my mind love?

You know I was or you would not have spoken to me in there
and said things that you knew would make me smile, Runa
proclaimed. Then she took off her cloak which is all she ever
wore, not that she ever had any other clothing to wear but
I liked her naked it seemed natural to me. We slept.

Days passed and still we waited for Bob or Japo to tell us news
of our hiding foe, it didn't come. Justin popped out onto a
asteroid not far from where we were. He was thinking of his
children and his mates and of Jeanie who did not know about the
kids or other women. He looked at me as I materialized beside
him. We looked at each other without a spoken word, I just
patted him on the back and smiled, the rest he already knew so it
didn't need to be said. We sat there for hours staring out into the
stars, trying to find out what purpose our lives had or if we would
loose and our kids would die as a result.

For the first time Justin knew what it felt like to be a parent
and worry.

The days passed and the hours dragged by as we waited for
our omniscient friend to come out and answer the burning
question, where is our enemy, when can we get him and finish
our business, so we can go home again which had been a long
road for me. After months of waiting Japo came forth and so did
Bob. They were had from the mental battle that they were
waging for months and had to win, yet they smiled.

279

SHANE

The tale was weaved over the food that they had not had in two months and some days. Goth was hold up in a familiar place, the hall of portals so he could jump into one if we started to win the battle for time and space. It was not a wise place for him to choose I thought. In his haste he has finished himself. I knew what plan would work now and how we would be back with our loved ones in no time. I started laughing crazy and all the others looked at me like I was loosing it but they didn't say it because I had seen much more pain and suffering from this than all the others combined.

I am laughing because Goth has sealed his fate and I who am Destiny (my voice thickened until it was thunder) will send that bastard to his final rest my friends. I have a plan that will require you to travel with me to see some old friends who are in my debt, and even if they were not they would still help me take out Goth. They looked at each other for a moment, then they looked at me and agreed to do whatever I demanded to carry out my plan for a photo finish. I explained the plan in parts, some in stages so they could be clearly engaged and locked up.

First, we go to see a troll of great power, who is sworn to Destiny as long as he lives.

I waved my hand and all of the people in Fect's house but him were transported to the land of Bnurr the troll, wizard who was as old and wise as they came if you overlooked his greed.

We approached his gate and there was a formidable force barrier there. I had to smile because I knew that this was put there

SHANE

because of what happened to him the first time I visited him. I walked through the barrier to the other side where I found him hard at work in his laboratory on some unknown experiment. He did not turn around but I thought he realized that I was there he just hoped I would go away.

Hello old Bnurr troll, I said to him in a flat voice that I knew would not startle him incase he did not know I was there.

He must have not known because he turned fast and almost dropped his work.

Another one of you in one week I don't believe what rotten stinking luck I am having lately, he said. Well I know that you are Destiny for sure because the other guy, a bald one said that you would come and destroy me if I did not splash that shit over there in the bucket on ya, but I know it would not work, so his real purpose was to make you distrust me, he explained in great detail.

Do you think that I trust you Bnurr, I asked?

You know that I gave my word to serve you as long as I live, so I know that you trust me Destiny, the question is what you came to ask of me? What can an old troll like me do for you, he asked?

I want you to guard a portal that leads to the hall of portals, so that the bald guy you met earlier cannot escape me through it, I told him. I know that you don't think that that your powers are enough to turn him back, but they are and I will grant you some

SHANE

extra power to make sure that old chrome dome doesn't get by you, besides I will be on his heel no matter where he tries to go, I expanded. Now drop you defense grid so my friends can get in here to meet you.

He complied and they came in.

This handsome young man is my son, who happens to be Lord Justice by the way. To his right is Bob my friend who is the Key of Truth and his mentor.

Japo the Kim, the troll answered before I said it.

I smiled at Bnurr who was smiling for the first time since I met him at Japo.

That is correct he is a universe council member, but how did you know that Bnurr.

I am the oldest living troll in the known universe and have met Japo more than once in my life, he said still smiling at his old friend.

Good, then on to the last member of the visiting party, Mistress Hope who is also my love, I told the troll who was soundly enjoying the visitation. He told me that anything he could do, he would, just give him the instructions. I told him his part of the plan and he committed it to his memory, then we sat down to lunch in the sun and feasted hardily.

SHANE

We left the home of Bnurr the troll having set him to his task and
leaving him in the best mood of his later life. We were off on our
journey to the castle of Firewitchs to seek the aid of my old
friend Pyro and his bride princess Sky. As we neared the giant
castle we were intercepted by a platoon of airborne Firewitchs
who pulled down on us. The fire that they shot was well in front
of us as a warning not to come any farther or they might be
forced to strike at us instead of in front our path. I laughed and
so did everybody else as the leader landed and said his well
prepared speech.

Go back, the castle is off-limits to all but Firewitchs strangers, he
said sternly.

 I am sure you needed to say that but I am always welcome at
the castle no matter what is happening, I said with a curt smile.

The Firewitch raised his hand to cast and another told him to
wait as he grabbed his wrist.

 Who are you sir the second Firewitch asked?

 I am Destiny. Your King and Pyro are sworn to my service if I
have need of them, I said.

They looked hard at me then at each other.

 Aren't you glad that you didn't try to fry him now or your
bones would be fertilizing the country side at this moment,
the second witch said as he bowed to me. We will take you right

283

SHANE

to the king Lord Destiny , I am sorry for the delay in our
service to you, he said.

   WE followed them into the castle where some of the people
remembered the man who came with titans in his service and
told the rest of the folks that were gathering to see who was
admitted to the castle. The guards looked scared as they
recognized me when I walked past and stopped turned and said,
relax men I am a friend remember. We resumed to the chamber
of the Fire King. The doors swung in and there he was sitting on
his thrown when we walked through the doors into the room. He
jumped to his feet and stared at the guards.

   I said no visitor during this time, he yelled at the guard
who was shivering in fear of both the king and I.

   I think you should be glad to see me you fat old butcher, I said in
fun when he looked up.

It all came to him in a flash as he realized whom was addressing
him. His face went white as he remembered the awe inspiring
powers that I had at my disposal and he was being rude and
unfriendly.

   You didn't even write home when you were away, and I didn't
know you were coming he said as he was groping for a good
story for the treatment I had received by his hands. Sky is with
child and it goes bad Sean, she dying and I can't do a damn thing
to help her, he told us as the tears began to fall from his
massive regal form.

284

SHANE

I turned to Runa and she knew that I wanted her to tend to Sky. She followed a guard to the room where Sky laid dying. I could hear Pyro yelling at Runa but he suddenly appeared next to me and he stopped yelling.

I told him that the women that was tending to Sky was Runa the key of Hope and that she would heal her and that she has had children so everything is going to be okay.

The time went by at a very slow pace because there was no news and nobody was allowed in the room while Hope weaved her magik medicine for Sky. Four hours later Hope came out of the room carrying a baby boy in her arms that she walked up and put it in Pyro's hands.

This is your son Pyro, look into his eyes and tell him your his father and then the baby will sleep in peace, Hope said. O' by the way Sky is fine, the baby was just breached so I flipped him around, she added then snapped her fingers as to say it was nothing.

The moment was filled with joy as everyone crowded Pyro to look at the newborn baby Firewitch. He had tiny little wings and smoke coming from his finger tips. All things considered this was a terrific elf. I left the group to check on Sky who was more than likely spent from the ordeal of trying to have a breach baby. However, when I arrived at her door she was getting dressed and noticed me.

285

SHANE

Well don't just stand there, you have seen me naked before come in, she cracked. Sky was wearing only her necklace when she turned herself around and walked up and wrapped her arms around me, kissing me firmly. I am glad to see you again Sean, Runa told me that you sent her to me when the baby was out of position so you are our savior once again, she told me in an almost singing voice. We, Pyro and I have decided that the boy will be named Sean like you because without you we would never have come together in the first place, Sky said with pride.

I heard footsteps coming this way so I told Sky that the future queen must not be seen naked all the time, so she should dress. Smiling she kissed me again and dressed quickly before anyone reached the door and was sitting with me when they did appear. Pyro's big grinning face was the first to grace the room, he was followed by the rest of the party, who came to see Sky, mother of a future king. Runa came right over and sat by me letting her cloak fall open which brought plenty of attention in nothing flat. I traveled around with her but sometimes I forgot how incredible she is from head to toe until I see the looks on other men's faces at her naked torso.

You did good Runa, all of the fire kingdom is in celebration now that lil' Sean has been born, I said.

She just smiled and kissed me, hugging me tightly against her breasts. I didn't want to stop but we were there to get help trapping Goth and ever second wasted was another second that could be spent in the arms of a loved one back on Lon.

SHANE

I told the king and Pyro that I needed to speak with them about important matters when they could brake away. They told me that after they presented the boy prince to the people that their time was mine no matter how long I needed.

The crowd that was gathered below the balcony of the royal ballroom was staggering, there must have been a million or more fire folk. The king went on the balcony and raised his hands, the crowd fell silent and then Pyro and Sky walked out carrying baby Sean which filled me with pride.

People of the Fire Kingdom you have a new member to the royal family, said the king as he turned to Pyro and Sky.

They walked up the rail of the balcony and held up the baby. This is your new prince baby Sean who was named after Lord Destiny our dearest friend. The baby squirmed at that moment and he fell from Pyro's grasp. A guard from the ground ripped into the air at a devil speed, Pyro dove hard instantly after his baby, but I knew that both Pyro and the guard would be to late so I raised my hand as did all the keys. but I didn't notice at that time.

Take wing baby Sean you can fly, I said as I cast a beam of pure light on the child.

His lil' baby wings opened and he stopped and hovered right there flapping his baby size wings. All the crowd cheered and Pyro brought the baby back to the balcony where he noticed that all four of the Keys were glowing.

287

SHANE

I don't know who I am supposed to thank you are all glowing from magik, said Pyro. WE all looked at each other and laughed, this was a good sign that we would do well in combat together, because we think fast and alike.

We all except your thanks, but I think you might find that since we all juiced the baby, he might develop extra abilities such as healing or telepathic talents, I told him.

Everyone was pleased and the king said he would meet us in the war room for whatever we needed to talk about.

The room was quite rich in-leu of it's purpose and the chairs were big comfy bucket seats. The king can in followed by Pyro and Sky, the baby flew through the doors as they were closing sideways. Sky held up her hands but he passed her and came in for a landing on my lap with a baby giggle.

Bob said well what'cha know about that, I guess he must already know who's name he has. And some of Big Sean's powers to boot just to top it off, he added. Sky and Pyro seemed surprisingly pleased at this development, but none as much as the baby who was playing with my fingers.

I think this meeting should come to order, I said with a smile at the baby. I have come here with my fellow keys to enlist your help against my enemy Goth. He is the one who pulled me into the rifts in time and cause me to become Destiny.

288

SHANE

A big ball headed fool perhaps, said the king? He was here not long ago telling that a powerful enemy would come to destroy us and take Sky's baby, that is why the extra security was in place. I think he was trying to turn you against us for some reason, the king ventured.

Justin said the reason is that your one of dad's powerful allies and Goth needs to make sure in the final conflict your not with him, or on his side secretly. Justin's look at the king was not of friendship but of stern judgment. I observed the king's eyes drop to the table, but I didn't interrupt Justin because I wanted to see where this would lead. Did you tell Goth that you would double cross us, did you!

Yes, father what of this, did you say these lies to our friend's enemy or to our friends, Sky growled at her father through eyes a blaze with anger? Pyro calmed Sky but he never took his eyes off of the king because he want to hear the answer as much as the rest of us did, more since he was to be king.

The king looked as though he would cry but Truth comforted him so he could say what he had to.

There is no need to be ashamed of your actions because I see the Truth in your heart, Bob said to the king who bucked up.

Yes, I told that bald madman that I would help him but I would say anything to get him to leave Sky's baby alone, the king explained.

289

SHANE

WHAT, said Pyro as he lost his seat for his feet?!

Sit down as I tell you the whole story. Goth came to me a week ago and told me of great danger, that Destiny would return and that he wanted me to destroy him. I refused, Destiny is my friend I told him, he only shook his head. Then he said it is the death of destiny or of Sky's baby you choose king of nothing, before I could kill him he was gone but Sky was suddenly in great pain and I thought that he was reminding me that my choice must be made. So I picked the lives of my little girl and the baby, can you fault me for that?

There is no evil in you sir said Hope and I made a similar choice not long ago if I remember, she looked at me and smiled. You have a new chance now to make right what is wrong, are you with us, she said?

I am twice beholden to you for saving something near my heart, I am old and have lived badly at times but I swear that my life is yours to take or command as you will, said the Fire King as he pulled a knife and cut his hand, in my own blood I make this oath!

Very well, then this is what I need from your Firewitchs, I answered. I told him that in the coming battle against Goth I wanted him to guard a portal or more to make sure Goth can not escape me through one. The king was happy to be going to battle once more. One more thing Goth has powerful demons and Titans in his service so you all must fight for your lives in the final conflict there will be no waiting around involved.

SHANE

Pyro said we can't handle titans without you, but demons beware for we will crush them.

I am aware that your not powerful enough for titan fighting so we will give your people extra power, to even the fight in that case, also you will have titan allies from Ger's and Windrider's peoples to back you up, I told them. Pyro will be in absolute command and the titans know of you and will obey you because of your bravery and Ger's order to. Pyro was pleased at the thought of his own titan warriors.

The hours went by as the plans were made and a curt strategy was formed to think through all the possible scenarios that could pop up during the course of the upcoming conflict. When all the preparations were made then we said our farewells and set once more in search of another old friend to help guard the portals, so in the end Goth would have to face me and be put to rest for good.

We left the Fire Kingdom behind us and went on the trail the would eventually lead us home. It was the land of dragons that we now headed for to find Kel and Mony, to see if they to would throw in with us.

I walked the same path as before remembering the nights that Mony and I cooked over an open fire, told jokes and stories just to pass the time. How different it seemed now that I had to asked them, all my friends everywhere to wage war for not just themselves but for all of creation. We could not fail in this fight, to fall short meant that Goth would rules all the universe, and he

SHANE

is a madman. My thoughts served to strengthen my resolve in my approach to ending this mess and setting right all that was undone by the evil fool we chased. There was no doubt that he was lying in the weeds for us but that trap would be unsprung if I had my way.

 A villager in the road saw us coming and said call out the guard, strangers approach, danger, danger! I looked at my friends who just shrugged their shoulder and smiled. We moved down the road and into the village where lots of houses were recently vacated, there was no one around. A thundering sound from behind us cause our attention to shift from the empty homes to the shaking ground. The sounds and shaking ground were caused by four dragons who were ridden by men and they were charging right at us with no warning.

Justin put his hand on my shoulder and said one word, Mine with a smile.

I nodded and he went into the road forty feet in front of us and just stood there, but he was starting to glow. The dragons ran into him and the outer two flipped on their sides, the unfortunate middle two were stopped dead by Justin's hands which sent the riders in flight.

   I walked over to one of the men trying to get off the ground and said, are you okay buddy, you took a nasty spill?

The man just looked at me and tried to get up but his legs were broken badly. Just relax pal and we'll fix your legs for you.

292

SHANE

Meanwhile Bob and Justin were tending and mending the other one including the downed dragons.

Your not going to be laughing when Lord Kel finds you, he will kill you for what you've done to us, the man said.

First of all bud, you attacked us and second we are healing your dumb asses, third since I am the one who gave Kel those powers, I'll take them away if he abuses them, now hold still until I finish mending your arm, I said to him.

He regarded me carefully but didn't say anything else while I mended his body.

We finish healing them and they got up and left without a word, almost if they were afraid to speak even one more word. The road was clear so we continued on it until we reached the town where Del Tar lived. Unlike the town before this village was not afraid of us and some of the people waved hello. We waved back and tossed coins of their type to them so that they would be happy we came even if it was to bring war. We went to the center of town which was the arena, that is where we found Del Tar training young men to fight.

Del Tar a word with you please I said, he didn't even answer. I grew to the size of a titan and reached down and picked Del Tar up, I said I want to talk with you.

He did not miss a beat.

293

SHANE

You've grown since I last seen you Sean, he said wryly.

I reduced to my normal size and put Del on the ground. He was glad to see me and asked us to have lunch with him at his house. We agreed and took off for his dwelling. When we arrived the people were a little scared because they knew I was Destiny and were scared I might blast them or something. After the servants laid out the meal, Del Tar told them to leave so we could talk alone in piece. I told him why I was there and he told me the story of what had transpired in this world when I had left.

As it turned out Kel was still a boy and was afraid to use his powers unwisely, so some unsavory men started telling him what he should do and they have poisoned the boys mind to anyone but them. They take what they want and live off of our blood and sweat, I have been training these men to overthrow those tyrants, said Del Tar.

There is no need for that, I will take care of Kel's little problem, but what about Mony, I asked?

The dragon has kept the kid from going off the deep end but has sworn to protect Kel and can't leave him with those bastards or all our butts would be in the ringer. They have tried to kill Mony several times but he is indestructible and always kills the assassin.

I told him we would go and fix the damage that was done by evil hands.

294

SHANE

The next morning we were at the palace that Kel built for himself and Mony, yet they were not living there but this trashy bunch of scum were, so Justin and Bob put out the trash while I searched for Kel and Mony. I found them by the lake I made when I was here before skipping stones.

Hello Kel and greetings Mony, I said.

Kel wheeled around and the ground at my feet rose up and engulfed me like a cocoon. I have seen this before I thought, I waved my hand and the dirt fell to the ground. Kel cast again and lightning crashed down on me, but dissipated one foot from me.

Mony get him said Kel!

NO, Your wrong and he is our friend, and on the best day of our lives we could not hope to even scratch his skin, said Mony!

Kel just looked at the dragon, then at me.

Yeah, your right, that bald guy said if I beat you I get your powers, but that's dumb because if I could beat you I would not need your powers, said Kel in shame.

I walked over to him and said your in need of some good advice really bad I hear.

I took him to the palace where he noticed his councilors laying on the lawn in pain.

SHANE

 I told him that we through the trash out, so that the light could find it's way back into his life.

 We all sat down and I told Kel who everyone was, then I told him what it was I came for. He looked a little surprised but Mony didn't, who sat on the floor smiling at the thought of being of great help to the whole universe, we'd be heroes.

Kel agreed because he didn't have a choice as he saw it, help or maybe be lost forever if Goth won.

I told him that Del Tar would help train everyone and that Titans and Firewitchs would also come to his aid before we engaged Goth.

 The plan was made clear to Kel and Mony before we left and Del Tar told Kel that any advice from now on was going to come from a real man, namely himself.

 Hope transported us to the world where my old friends and super powerful allies were, Ger and Windrider. When we got there they were waiting for us and said that anything it took to whip Goth we had. Further, Ger told me that he had contacted Pyro and titans were already sent to back him up just incase anyone was dumb enough to try to break free there.

I told Ger that I needed titans of Windrider's clan to act as support for Kel in Dragon world.

SHANE

No problemo amigo, said a raspy voice behind me. I knew it was Rider but I acted dumb anyway.

Who said that, I asked?

Windrider only laughed and someone I also knew came forth. Lok, but what is he doing here, this is the wrong world for him to be in.

I called to Windrider the way you did that day years ago and he came to me. I told him the story of my world and the scar on my hand. He said the scars and your blood gave me powers that I didn't know I had, even if they were modest, they were enough to raise a titan to my side. I have been here every since and I have made many powerful friends, he explained.

What is the extent of your abilities Lok, I asked?

He gave me a demo of them one at a time. First he could throw fire like a firewitch, second he could fly, third he could move things with a thought no matter how big which he show by lifting Ger, who was forty stories tall.

Good show, your talents are needed elsewhere, I said as I touched him, now your invulnerable as well. He smiled.

Your not looking to bad brother, but the sadness is still about you. However, I see you brought some sunshine with you, he said looking at Runa.

SHANE

Ger said that he did not need many titans to guard his gate
because he and Rider were the most powerful titans hands down,
could do It alone, so he could send his titans anywhere I wanted.

I thought about it and suggested that they enter the hall of
portals and guard the known gates from the inside, more eye and
ears the better to capture Goth and his lot.

WE planned for two more days while Runa and the others
explored Ger's world. We were joined by Pyro and Kel that
afternoon for some fine tuning of the battle plan. Later the troll
Bnurr came through a portal of his creation into the room, gave
his greetings then sat and joined in the planning.

I told them that I had two more sets of allies to bring to the fight
so I must leave to fetch them to this assembly.

I went through the portal alone this time looking for my friends
in the desert, but it was not a desert now, I stood on top of a
small hill looking down on Eden. The sheer beauty of it brought
tears to my eyes. I stood there just absorbing the grace of God's
world as shaped by Havax.

Seer was waiting for me. I followed him to the palace of the
Shama, Dear lovely little Havax. When I came in the meeting hall
it was full of familiar faces which were all happy at my arrival.
I walked up to the steps of the throne where Havax sat and she
jumped off of it into my arms. The crowd roared.

I missed you she said and she kissed me lovingly again and

SHANE

again still wrapped around me. She told me that it had been peaceful since I left and now the I was back she wanted to show the world to me. I smiled but didn't say anything.

I sat on the steps with Havax in my arms still and I said did Seer tell you why I came back and what I want you to do Havax. She shook her head that she knew. As I scanned the rest of my friend and warriors they also knew why I had come and they were ready. I think I would like to see some of your new world.

Seer knew that it was because it may not be so beautiful when the fighting is over, but he said nothing.

WE walked over the country side and Havax said your my mate you know, that means that I can only have offspring with you. She looked so sad. I said in that case we should work on a child. She looked at me with wanting searching eyes. I thought that this land is the perfect place to start a family since it is so green and fertile. I led Havax to a spot by a small river, pilled some leaves and laid down on them after shedding my cloths. WE made love all day and part of the night and when we were finished we washed off in the creek that was nearby.

I am with child Sean, Havax said, I know because It already begins to grow inside of me at a quicker than normal rate because I am over charged with life energy. WE dried off got dressed but we took our time going back to the great hall to just enjoy the life we felt at that moment. At the great hall where there council was waiting for us to give them the orders, Seer

SHANE

had already told them the plan and the cost of loosing. Some of them were afraid but, Still they were ready to go to the war meeting being held in the titan hall when I left.

I said I need to go to one more ally before we are set to take down Goth, I will meet you in titan hall.

Meanwhile, Justin went to Roden and Nutm with the Rat folk and asked them to join also. Roden was pleased to be of help and Nutm said that he had know this battle was coming for many centuries and that it was the Rat folks duty to help anyway they could. Justin took them to titan hall to await my return and the start of end game.

My path led me to Durn my powerful pirate friend and the ladies of Lon who were extremely powerful telepaths. I greet them both with a hardy hug then we sat down over a cup of nectar, I began to weave my tale for them of Goth. Sira and Durn listened to me with out a word then they both agreed that helping me was the only coarse of action that could take.

I went to my house and Mira and Sira came there too. We all climbed into my bed and held each other as if for the last time, then we made passionate love until the three of us were totally exhausted. We fell into a coma like sleep but there were no dreams for me.. When I woke up my children were crawling all around me, playing with my face and my fingers.

I played with them for hours then I said see you babies later. I found Sira and Durn and told them that we must all join the

SHANE

others in the titan hall shortly. Durn told me anytime I was ready so was he and his crew.

That's fine Sean, I have a surprise for you, an old acquaintance has asked to join the fight. Prylor Lasget stood just in front of me smiling. He is offering to help what do you think?

How can you be of help Lasget in our battle, I asked?

He smiled, then he vaporized my chair with a look from his eye which was solid white as he worked, but went back to normal after he was demonstrating. I think that should answer your question quite nicely he said smiling at me.

I agreed that his help and his people was going to be a bonus that I did not count on. I still explained the whole show to him so he would be sure or not if this was a good idea for the Cyclops. Lasget told me that their race had been in many wars and had special armor to protect them from harms way. We departed with a handshake and a curt farewell to Sira.

We arrived at the titan hall and everyone was quiet, the plans were finished and everyone knew the plan. Hope cast a magik symbol on all of our allies everywhere so we would know a friend from an enemy, but only friends could see the symbol.

Well my friends the final hour awaited is now upon us and there is no turning back, it is Goth or us, there can't be a tie or we start all over again. Further, should Goth escape we have to start again and that would be devastating. Now let's go get that son

SHANE

of a bitch.

 The hall of portals was very dark when we entered, so we were
lowing at full power from the get go. Hope was shining as white
as the falling snow, and Bob was shining a nice orange color,
Justin was silver and gold, lastly I was a deep fiery blood red. WE
walked into the room where Vapor's thrown was and there was
some demons at the foot of it. They were holding magik weapons
that were no danger to us, but might give some of the troops
problems. We continued to approach the thrown and even more
demons reared their heads, it was apparent to us that hall was
saturated with demons that we have to get rid of if we were to
nab Goth. The demons did not seem to want to get to close to us
because they knew who we are and didn't really want to die
earlier than normal.

 Where is Goth demon said Justice as he vaporized ten demons.
Tell me or it will cost ten more until one of you talk, now
spill it or else, added Justice.

None spoke and ten more went to the promised land. Now speak
of Goth or next I'll do fifty, said Justice. Still no demon would
talk, so Justin started mowing them down without another word,
until there were only a few left.

 Justice was about to obliterate the remaining demons when
I said hold.

 WE will set you demons free to go home if you tell us where
Goth is, I said, you have the word of Destiny?

302

SHANE

O' master Destiny we can not tell you because Goth holds our souls and will send them to limbo if we talk, said the demon.

Truth said he was telling the truth and waved his hands toward the demons and the souls were regained by them. I have restored your souls to you, now if you please, where is Goth, asked Truth.

He is in limbo waiting for you to assemble the Key to the Universe, answered the demon. They dropped their weapons and Truth transported them home.

We thought for a moment, he would never really share his plans, so he was around here somewhere. I started down a side hallway followed by the other keys when a demon jumped on me and took my key from around my neck, then dove through portal only to come face up on Pylor Lasget who blasted the demon and tossed my key back through, then followed it through and stood guard on that portal from the inside now. It was obvious that Goths plan was to get our keys and assemble the big key to bring back his former life.

Hope noticed some noises down a sublit hallway and we went to investigate them. When we got there we were faced by two titans who looked pissed off about something.

You killed Vapor our friend and leader now we're gonna kill you, one titan said then charge us.

303

SHANE

The moment was as tense as I had ever lived because titans are extremely powerful and hard to kill without blasting the area that they occupy to atoms and them with it. Just as they got about close enough to strike, four of Ger's clan stepped from the shadows and pulled the other titans into a portal.
They returned only moments later covered in blood.

It's okay master Destiny, the blood isn't ours, said the smallest of the lot with a large smile. I saluted them our thanks. They now stood guard at that corner corridor so that no one but a friend could follow.

The plan seemed to be working way to well to be real, I thought to myself. Hope told me that she was feeling very misled by the events that were unfolding, she believed that Goth wanted us to think it was going to be easy to lull us into a false sense of comfort. I didn't think any of us felt secure at the moment, and we all were ready for a to-the-death type scene and if anything were a little disappointed. We travel a little farther and Truth told us that Goth was killing some of the desert planet people right now.

I yelled at the titans don't let anyone follow us, they waved. We stepped into the nearest portal and we were in the thick of the battle, we thought we would have to fight.

Goth was leading his troops right down on Havax's forces which were holding their own but there were allot of dead.

Windrider I need you, I thought to myself and the air burst

SHANE

into flames. Windrider and ten more of his clan shot into the
light and landed in front of me. I just pointed and he nodded.

The titans went right to work on our enemies, killing them.

The battle was joined by Lok who began to cut the demon horde
to pieces in a rage I did not think he could reach. Havax was
using the ground itself to defeat the invading army, and they
were winning until thousands of evil titans showed up then it was
Lok's turn to bleed. Windrider saw Lok downed by a titan, so he
turned and flew right through Lok's attacker killing him instantly.
He picked up Lok and took him and Havax who was also hurt to
safety while the four of us keys entered the fight.

So you sorry bastard want to play rough huh, okay try this, I
yelled then I cast and millions of razor sharp rocks cut right
through them killing most of them instantly.

The one who tried to run away turned right into Justice who had
no pity and sent them to express mail to the maker.

Wrong choice boys he said as a beam of light shot from his
hands, incinerating anything it touched. And some even escaped
Justin but dared not try to fly away even if they had wings
because nine out of the ten members of Windrider's clan were
still in the air, the death from above you might say.

Just when it looked like we might be winning Goth called
in the rest of his minions. Dear God, Bob said there are more
of them than I have ever seen. Truly we were hopelessly out

SHANE

numbered.

 Hope said call all of our friends here now for this is truly the final battle.

 Firewitchs, space pirates, and winged titans blotted out the sun as they approached. It looked like the end of the world, only this was for the universe. Prylor and his people shot from ever portal and their armor shined as they covered the field like ants. It was like Lasget told us, their armor would protect them from harm, because they jumped demons and titans equally without any sign of hesitation. They were a mighty force to be reckoned with.

 The battle was still in the favor of the evil foe, we were not at full strength yet, but Goth didn't know that and he came close enough to yell at me. He got my attention by blasting me in the back, but it only staggered me and I turn on him.

 Your forces are loosing the war and soon I will be the ruler of the galaxy, Destiny, he scoffed. I think soon you will call me master boy, and I will have you whores to as play things I think, he added just to piss me off. I blasted him right out of the sky. He hit the ground like a ton of bricks and when he looked up I was right over him ready to finish my job. I got hit by a fist as big as a Mack truck, and flew across the battle field and landed right in front of an enemy titan who reached down to grab me. He should have been watching because Ger grabbed his head and ripped it off of his shoulders.

 Are you well master, you took quite a shot from that rock

SHANE

giant over there, Ger asked me. Would you like me to get you
to safety Sean, or just watch your back as you fight, he said.

Watch my back so the next time I get Goth in my sights I can
finish him off, I said in a rage. I wasn't going to let out my spirit
because that much power is hard to re-harness and it is a terrible
thing to behold, but this battle was going badly for the Firewitchs
and desert people who were dying fast.

Suddenly, I heard the sound of singing, it was Kel and Mony and
they had every damn dragon in their world, plus a crap load of
good fighters with blood in their eyes. All singing at the top of
their lungs, as one united battle cry.

The battle started to swing but still we were out numbered.
That's when the Rat folk and the Witch-women of Lon showed up.
Roden told his men to kill anything that did not have our mark on
it. And believe me when I say that those rat were some kind
of fighters, they were killing with their bare hand, arrows,
swords, and magik. Titans could not even resist their
unbelievable onslaught. Roden led the blood thirsty Ratmen to
the far side of the fight pushing our enemies in. Lasget was on
the near side doing the same thing. They must have discussed
this earlier incase it was an option. Our enemy was still strong
but nowhere near as well trained or organized.

Mira led the Witch-women into battle and I was worried that
they would be slaughtered. They were using psionic blasts to
kill their opponents, so that's why nobody could conquer them.
Sira told her women to help Lasget's cyclopean to hem in the

SHANE

enemy. We had the whole of Goth's forces inside a perimeter, where we could cut them to pieces in the crossfire. That is exactly what we did.

In the sky above Rider with the pirates, Firewitchs, and the dragons led by Mony were bring a hell of firepower down on the crowd below. The end was near now and we would finish Goth and his evil army. Well I was right about the end of the battle, but I was dead wrong about Goth. He was gone.

The last of Goth's army were surrendering to Ger when we noticed no evil leader. I looked around and Seer and Truth were talking about something.

Hey where is Goth, tell me, I said.

I don't know was all they knew to tell me. Sean where is your key, I thought as I touched my neck. That's it Goth didn't want to win by force, he was winning by craft. He stole my damn key, clever I thought to off balance me by faking the show of force and fingering the key. I almost admired the bastard for a moment.

Truth, Justice, and Hope where are your keys I demanded? They all felt their necks at the same time and there were no keys under their hands. It was all for nothing I thought, the war, the dead and the journey, for nothing now that he had our keys. I turned, Fect and Japo were standing behind me with the master key.

308

SHANE

It is not finished until Goth places your key on the master, until then it is not over my son, said Japo.

Fect gave me the master key and said Goth is waiting for this in the hall of portals, so take it to him.

I stood regarding him for a long time before I made any movement at all. Then I just shook my head in agreement and turned toward the portal. Ger was sitting in the grass holding Lok who was really bad off and loosing the will to live when I walked up to them. His body was torn apart. You could see his heart beating and lungs because his chest was ripped open, He looked up at me.

I never gave an inch, never backed up, I went forward with your courage in my heart brother. I am dying and I can laid down satisfied that in the end I was worthy of you might friendship and trust he choked out through blood dripping lips.

Tears fell freely from my eyes, what had I ever done to deserve this man's un-flinching loyalty. He placed my needs before his very life. I put my hand over Lok's face and said this gift I give to you and I pulled away my hand. Lok sat up looked at me and smiled. Ger stopped me as I turned to leave.

I will go with you master, as will Rider, if you wish to watch your back, he said. I know this is your duty, but I know also that Goth will cheat if he can, so I must go to watch your back for assassins, Ger said with much conviction. I looked into his heart and I saw that I was the only one of his friends other than Rider

SHANE

that he would give his life for. I smiled shook my head no, with great regret. Looked around at the grief stricken faces staring back at me, with hope, courage and love, and lastly pity then simply turned and left with no ado.

 The hall was brightly lit this time when I entered it. I was sure I could feel Goth ahead of me in the thrown room. He was right there sitting on the chair smiling at me like we were long lost old friends.

 You've had a hard fight and a long journey, but now all you have to do is give me the master key Sean and we all get to go home, Goth said in a very friendly manner. It was I, was it not that sent you to find the key for me, and you did now, let me have it, he casually stated. He looked me up and down to see if I was buying it, but I don't think he knew because I was not going to give him anything. No way in hell was I going to give up the master key!

 Why go through the big show, when you could have just gotten the key for yourself or had a demon do it for you, why drag me into this crazy mess, I asked while carefully watching him?

 Simple, my old friend Fect was not going to let me or a demon near that key, you see he is not just an old councilman he is the old Destiny, Sean and would only give the key to you, he told me.

 I knew that he just told the truth, but I still didn't think I heard the whole story yet.

SHANE

I will also tell you this, that when you give that key to me you don't have to be Destiny anymore, he added.

That was the truth again only I knew the part that he left out this time and that was I would be dead.

Say I give you the key, what then, do I get to live the life I have made for myself in the last decade, or are you going to kill me and the rest of the Key masters, because I know that once your a key you are always the key, I told him.

His face changed to a more serious expression, this told me he was thwarted. I could blow you away now if I wanted to, what do you say to that, I asked?

He answer was plain to see, we were done talking. What I didn't know was that I had been talking to a hologram and that Goth was right behind me. He knocked the master key out of my hand, blasted me from behind and dove on the floor to get the key. He quickly assembled it with the four power keys and had the Key Of The Universe in his hand.

Now I am the ruler of the universe he yelled at me and you have failed, now die insect. He pointed a finger at me and was about to end my existence.

A blast ripped the arm of Goth right off, ironically the one holding the key.

You forgot something Goth once you assembled the key in you

SHANE

hands, you were human again and can die, said Bnurr as he smiled at me. He blasted Goth again with his staff.

I picked up the Key and said," By the right of the good in me and by the stars in the sky, I send you Goth to the hell that God has judge for you". I looked at Goth as the great power from the key tore him apart and sent him to his reward. I looked at the old troll who was still smiling, what's so funny?

He said I don't like that titan Ger, but he gave you some good advice about watching your back son, and I told you that I would do what ever was necessary to help you and that is just what I done, he said. Oh, one more thing you are the ultimate power in the universe next to the creator who made it. Outside this place the universe is shifting meet your temperament, your wish is it's command so be careful of what you wish for master, said the very wise old troll.

Windrider told me once that you were one of the wisest being in existence, now I know why he said that old friend.

You know that you saved us all and you should be the keeper of the power by rights, I told him.

No, Sean that was always your Destiny since the day of your birth, to free the universe of Goth and his evil, Bnurr explained. Now let's go because everyone in the universe is terrified because the changes will make them think you lost the contest.

SHANE

The troll was of-course right, the universe was changing. And no, I was not on a parallel with GOD, and never would want that. No the worlds shift in temperament and some in structure to reflect my good heart, nothing more than that. GOD built perfection Goth stained that, I merely washed that stain away.

We walked through the portal and down the hill where everyone was waiting in fear. When they saw me they knew that the universe was whole again and we could all go home.

Cheers and tears fell like rain for many days to come at the news of our ultimate victory and the prospect of a new life for all.

All the heroes and friend gathered one last time to share their brotherhood and friendship before going on to rebuild their corner of the universe. Ger welcomed all to go home with him to live if any wished but everybody wanted to go home, to His or her own home for the first time in years.

There would be no rest for me, but I will take the time to go home at least once more before the real journey begins

SHANE

SHANE

PROLOGUE:

The lighthouse was foggy when I walked through the mist up to the door and knocked. The door opened and there was a young face looking out at mine. I was dressed head to toe in a long red robe with a bright blue hood like a monk from Tibet, I looked up and her eye began to water into big ocean tears, her arms fell over my shoulders and we embraced as two lovers long apart, reunited.

 I told her it was done but I could no longer stay on Earth because I had duties to perform throughout the universe. She cried harder.

 Then your going to leave me again, said the radiant young women?

    No, never again, never. I want you to come to Lon where I live now and stay with me, I said.

 Anything, anywhere, I'll go if I can be with you, Nicky said.

 We stood under the three suns on Lon as my children and there mothers greeted both of us, Runa explain who she was and who Mira and Sira were then took Nicky's hand and said will you stay and be our sister, raise the children and be one of us?

 Nicky looked at me then picked up Runa's son and said," Of-

SHANE

course this is my home now, with a heart felt smile...."

(THUS WE START A NEW ADVENTURE...OUR NEW LIFE)
(BUT THAT IS ANOTHER TALE)...

..THE END (FOR NOW)

...MAY YOU FIND YOUR KEY ...

.........W. SHANE WILSON ....

SHANE

SHANE

OTHER BOOKS BY THIS AUTHOR

BREATH OF MAGIK

ENTER THE GUARDIANS: KYL

VAMPIRE WARS

GUARDIANS : GROT

BLACK WINGS

BLOOD BY DAY